LONG LIVE THE KING

BOOK 1

CHRONICLES OF VENGEANCE

R.J. TAPSTER

Lowston Press

First Printing, 2021

ISBN: 978-1-9168925-1-4

For Serena
and Isaac

CONTENTS

PREFACE

This book is the first in the series 'Chronicles of Vengeance'... a series that was written to fulfil a primary purpose; a rescue. It's not easy to craft your own lifeboat when floundering in open water, so it's important that I thank those who have helped me get this far.

First, my wife. None of this would have been possible without your unwavering kindness and unfaltering support. Thank you for always being there, in so many ways.

Thank you also to my friends and family. I'd like to thank my brother for his constant company and support throughout a large portion of the years that have inspired these books. To my Dad for giving me an appreciation of the broader fantasy world from an early age. I want to thank my friends for being there for me in the last year, unknowingly pulling me out of a hole in fictional Eastern Europe.

I would like to thank Manowar and Dragonforce for introducing me to the beauty in the ridiculous that the fantasy world can provide. Final thanks go to my primary school teacher for writing these words in my year two school report; "Robert has trouble distinguishing fact from fiction" ... I should have recognised the positivity and possibility in these words many years ago, but I was only six.

I hope you like it.

1

SIMPLER TIMES

Jori was regarded as a good King. Though, as is often the case, those who serve under one King have very little comparison with which to measure their ruler's success. He was a strong leader and fair in his judgement. His achievements were great and their significance was never lost on his subjects. The Kingdom of Jorisham started and ended with King Jori; as the name suggests, the Kingdom and King were one and the same.

Jorisham is impressive, yet simple; consisting of one large walled city and a collection of outlying farms and villages. The city is a spectacle to behold. A sprawling network of clean, neatly bricked streets and clear blue waterways connected the diverse and comprehensive areas of the city together. The muscle of Jorisham comes from the industrial district, with the usual smokestack towers and heaving factories you would expect from a city so widely known for its exquisite manufacturing; from textiles to ironwork, Jorisham produced it all at a good rate and an even better standard.

King Jori knew that balance was the key to a thriving economy, so he countered the powerful industrial side of the city with a beautiful, green garden district. Twice as big as the city's muscles, the lungs of the city provided peaceful escape from the contrasting essential, yet busy work. The smallest, yet most celebrated district was the true artistic expression of the city; the artisanal lanes and alleyways of Lowston. Lowston did not obey the strict rules that governed the rest of Jorisham's infrastructure. Straight roads and efficiently planned factories were instead a twisting labyrinth of shops, bars, café's and above all… art.

As the expressive side of Jorisham, Lowston attracted all those who grew tired of the oppressive aggression of everyday life. Make no mistake, Lowston was no utopia, it was by far the poorest and most troubled of all the four districts. Along with attracting the most creative of Jorisham's citizens, it often attracted the most misguided and lost. Whilst the rest of the city struck a fine balance between nature and industry, work and recreation, Lowston was a fiery hotbed of imbalance. King Jori spent a little time in Lowston, but saw it more of a necessary evil than the 'Jewel in the City's Crown', as outsiders would remark. He allowed its presence and lawlessness in return for peace and stability in the rest of his city.

The fourth district sat raised above all others, on a hill in the middle of the city. The beating heart of Jorisham was home to the kingdom's elite in both the social and commercial sense. At the centre of this district was the royal castle; a walled city within the walled city. Walls that were unnecessary, with wide, open gates that reflected the nature of the ruling class within; all are welcome.

King Jori positioned the financial district next to the royal castle in order to keep a close eye on the commercial running of the kingdom; he had seen so many times before what could happen if a kingdom and its finances were not managed together. Jorisham was not the wealthiest of the five kingdoms, but it was not the poorest either. The kingdom and its people suffered hardships and times of prosperity the same as any other, but during his long reign, King Jori saw the kingdom rise from a small farming village to an imposing kingdom that almost all were proud of; but it was not always this way.

Before Jorisham, there were no kingdoms. It was not the first, but founded at the same time as all others. Before the formation of the five kingdoms as they are now known, there stood a collection of villages, towns and ports that existed in neither peace nor war. These were simpler times, with fewer people and less travel. Villages could exist for centuries without villagers ever meeting an outsider. Some villages grew naturally into towns, but even then, they were little more than large disorganised villages. One of these large villages was led by a man who would become King Jori.

Jori was a humble man, with an easy nature and strong drive. A drive that was unmatched by his fellow villagers, which allowed him to reach his status with relative ease. These times were distant enough for the details of how leaders like Jori rose to relative power to remain uncertain. As a result, history was passed down through stories, and King Jori was a keen story teller. This was especially true in his old age, when stories became subject to change on a regular basis.

Though the details are often unclear, the story remains consistent; these simple times were about to become complicated.

As for many of the nearby villages and towns, time stood still for Jori and those under his care. These honest, industrious people nurtured what they had and provided well for themselves, unaware of the activities of those that surrounded them; this made for a happy life, but one that could easily be taken away. For others, time was marching on, advancements were made and travel became simpler and swifter.

2

THE WINDS OF CHANGE

When the invading army arrived, their victories came easily. Until now, most villages had suffered squabbles and infrequent violent disputes: nothing that could have prepared them for an army of barbarians, organised and strong.

While villagers were tending land and using resources to provide security and growth, the barbarian hoards only had one focus... to take what they needed by force. One by one, the hoards tore through the scattered villages, recruiting willing men, imprisoning the women and children, then destroying the rest. It did not take long for word to spread to the larger towns, towns that were more advanced that Jori's.

By the time the Twelve leaders had assembled, more villages and towns, or their remains at least, belonged to the invading army than did not.

A meeting of this kind had never been possible before, and from it came a mixing of vastly different cultures.

Surrounded by powerful witches, wizards, industrialists and scientists, Jori felt unsure of his worth for the first time in his life. This leader of men, respected and loved by his people, could not think of a single useful addition that he could bring to aid their shared plight. The witches and wizards combined their powers, while the more advanced civilisations shared their knowledge and technology.

A plan was taking shape, with or without Jori, so when the council turned to him for his case to be made, he stumbled. "I... I am honoured to be amongst such esteemed and accomplished leaders. But, while I share the same enemy and have the same fears, I do not share the same abilities. I do not know any magic, I do not have any contraptions to help keep the barbarians away, I am just a farmer." Jori looked around, without any thought of what was to happen next, but with a vague hope of pity or assistance from one of the others.

"How did you come to be called to this council if you have no abilities or assistance to give?" sneered Vahvuus, one of the high witches from the South Eastern towns. Her sharp, angular features framed cold, light eyes that bore into him with contempt. "Surely you have a power, skill, or strength that allowed you to become such an esteemed leader? Well... esteemed enough for us to have heard about... Although admittedly not all of us." her face grew sour as she contemplated her own words. "It's almost as if we have an imposter among us, a leader who does not lead through merit, but theft. No better than a *barbarian*." Witches' words were notoriously cutting, as if by slicing open a wound, they were able to draw out what was buried beneath.

"I am no barbarian!" Jori bellowed. "I am where I am because of who I am! My people follow me because I lead them well! I have built all I have from the fruits of my hard labour and that of those around me!" He realised that he was standing and that his anger was visible, painted red across his face. He may not have been a tall man by any stretch, but when he was angered, he seemed to grow at least a foot. He sat down, taking a breath, and tried to compose himself. His voice began to mellow and his temper was easing. "My men would follow me to the ends of the earth if I asked, and I imagine many would follow me to their own deaths if I commanded it. So, don't you tell me that I do not deserve to rule my people.".

"Well, there we have it.", an elderly wizard mumbled from across the table. "The final piece in the puzzle. You shall command the armies that will defend the remaining free people of these lands." His demeanour was as soft as his voice, and this was the first time Jori had heard it. Nevertheless, his status and power were obvious from the response from of other leaders. Pensive yet confident nods were starting to lap around the large table.

"Well, that is agreed." said Millen, the industrial leader from the North-West. He was a tall, wide man with a thick auburn beard and wavy, thinning hair. "We shall need to meet regularly as a council in order to plan our defence against these invaders, I will set up lodging for all twelve leaders and halls for operations." Jori thought twice, but interjected anyway

"No, I'm sorry. This could be a long and drawn-out exercise and I... I can't be away for that long. I'm not undermining the severity of the situation, but I feel that-" the witch interrupted

"Oh, for goodness' sake, you have shown us that you are loyal to your subjects, you don't need to keep on about it." Again, Jori had to soften his approach, treading carefully among such powerful leaders; too much force and he could lose his tentative place at the council.

"My wife… fellow leaders. I could not do this without my wife. We have built our empire together and she has as much to add as I do. I would request that she joins me to aid our efforts."

"Oh…" said the large Northerner. "I will make arrangements to allow for this, if…" He looked around at the other council members, who all eventually nodded in reluctant agreement. "So be it. I look forward to meeting her".

Lowena was everything to Jori. One of the very few travellers from outside his town to enter its boundaries, she did so when it was still a village. To the people of the town, Jori and Lowena had been side by side since time began. In truth, she arrived shortly after Jori's village had combined with his neighbours, leaving Jori with a growing task. Lowena was the moon to Jori's Sun, the calm balance to his fiery passion. Whilst he was undoubtedly a remarkable man capable of impressive feats, Jori was flawed… as many men are.

If left unchecked, the very drive that made him successful would turn into rage. His strong will and determination could easily turn to stubborn bullishness, even in the face of logic. Not when Lowena was there. She managed without trickery or manipulation to calm the flames of his passion and to temper his will in order not to benefit herself, but to assist him in accomplishing what he needed to. Lowena was, above all else, humble. She allowed Jori the platform and status that his role required and needed none of the limelight for herself. She cared not for financial gain and spent much of her own personal time assisting others less fortunate. Lowena's heart belonged to those in need, and she felt that her purpose was

to assist them. She would have made the per
whilst she became one to so many who needed o
years, she was never blessed with children of her own.
love for Lowena was absolute, his tolerance of her pursuits
was wavering at times, but ultimately resolute. He knew that
her desire to help others was what made Lowena who she
was, and what kept her by his side.

3

THE WAR DRAGS ON

The council's operations were based in the centre of the combined lands. A place foreign to Jori and Lowena, but not unpleasant. The air was less rural than they were accustomed to, and the ground much cleaner. Hard, light bricks lined each street with fast, modern carriages gliding smoothly and silently on top. Since the council had set up in the area, a whole town had appeared around them. The busy traffic and urgent nature of their business within needed support. Transport in and out must be fluid, sustenance and refreshment must be readily accessible, and accommodation available for all those who were needed by the council. Once this was provided, more housing was needed for the workers providing these services. Manufacturing was moved into the new town for high priority items, and the combined land's financial operations were centralised in order to maximise efficiency. The assistance from the industrialists from the North-West and the scientists from the North-East led to innovations far beyond the comprehension of simple folk like Jori and Lowena. They were in awe of their new surroundings, yet comfortable within them.

While the council's endeavours against the barbarians were becoming more streamlined and efficient, they were getting no more effective. Modern communications allowed them to quell most invading attacks on villages, aside from the most remote ones; with Jori's armies able to swiftly advance from their strategic positions with the help of faster heavy-duty carriages.

It had been a year since the council was formed and on reflection, Jori could see that not being overrun by the barbarians and their slowly growing army was a victory. People were undoubtedly safer than they were prior to the council's efforts and the threat had been kept at bay to some extent, but something was gnawing away at Jori; a feeling of unease was taking hold.

"We can't do this forever, my love… it just won't last. I am throwing wave after wave of men at them but were not making any progress. Each time they invade, my armies get less and less and it's only a matter of time until the men see that. They are going to turn on me… I can feel it." Lowena put her hands on his shoulders and soothed his neck with her cold, gentle hands.

"You know that's not true. Your men will never turn. They love you like a father, you must be patient. Like the council says, we are stronger than them, not in force but as a unit. We own what we have, we grow it and we make it. Whatever those savages have, they must steal from us. If we stop them from taking what is ours, they will starve. This wait is painful for us, but it's much worse for *them,* believe me."

Again, Jori knew the wisdom in Lowena's words. He was reluctant to agree, but as always, he did.

"I suppose you're right, I just never thought it would take this long."

As the war waged on, Jori spent more time with the other council members, as did Lowena. Lowena would often spend her time ruminating with the wizards over the endless possibilities that magic could bring in helping the poor and diseased. The restrictions and limitations of magic left her both baffled and intrigued; *with such strong powers, how could they allow such suffering?*

Similarly, Jori spent much of his time plotting and scheming with the witches over how their magic could aid the struggle. Jori had men and he had desire, but what the witches had both frightened and excited him. Occasionally the council would allow some of their ideas to come to fruition and they yielded mixed results. An enchanted pack of enormous wolves helped keep one of the larger barbarian attacks from succeeding; until they turned on his own men once the invaders were dispatched. The forests of the far west were protected valiantly by the fire eagles they created until they burned it to the ground. They conjured powerful storms that hindered friend and foe alike, summoned magical beasts that could attack but not be controlled and created mystic weapons that gave great power to those who wielded them, but also those who stole them. It was too much risk.

"It's all about balance, Jori. You have all these ideas, but you don't think of the consequences. In magic, every positive needs a negative, whatever it gives, it must take away." Said Heilmur, the witch that he had become closest to. She was not the most powerful of the high witches, but she was the most agreeable, humouring Jori's naïve ideas and entertaining his grand schemes.

"Well then, what's the point?" sighed Jori, clearly growing less impressed with magic than he was initially.

4

THE TIDES TURN

It was autumn of the second year when their fates took a drastic turn. There had not been a barbarian attack for close to a month, which was considerably less than usual. Buoyed by the apparent weakness of the barbarian hoards, Jori attended the next council meeting with great anticipation.

"We have to strike now!" he exclaimed, failing in every way to cover his excitement. The others appeared to be less enthusiastic about the prospect than he was. This only made him more animated. "You have all got too used to sitting around and protecting what we have, celebrating when we defend with any success. Well... I say we attack. We need to reclaim what was taken from us and push them back to where they came from. If we don't do it now, we will regret it for years to come... this is our one chance!".

The council looked around, with not one member willing to voice the opposition that had become quite evident by this time. The council were wise and had become used to the fiery enthusiasm and strong will of the short army general, and they were very aware of the best way to deal with his nature.

"Lowena…" said Falmond, the soft, kind, elderly wizard that Lowena was closest to "…What do you think?" Lowena was, as always, sat on the edge of the council's meeting hall, along with financial consultants, messengers, and representatives from all over the combined lands, ready to give advice and offer detail when called upon. Although Lowena shared this position, she only did so at Jori's request, and had never been called to speak before.

"Me?" she stammered, knowing fully that the man she had come to know well, who had said her name and was starting directly at her… was in fact addressing her… along with the rest of the council, and a startled looking Jori. "I am… aware… of the err…." She paused to collect herself. "…We have been in the same position for some time now, and I can't see that it would be wise to let an opportunity like this pass. It has been the first time we have been given such a chance, and if there is the option of turning the tide in our favour, I agree that we should take it." She knew she had to stand behind her husband, there would be no coming back from such a public act of defiance, but she also knew that the council had turned to her for a more measured approach than their husband was giving. "However, I do not think that we should attack with full force. If they are planning something, we should tread carefully. We can't throw all our men at this, but we should still attack now that we have the chance." Jori sat a little taller. He always knew that Lowena supported him but his fears of an unlikely betrayal had been put to rest… They could not refuse now. "Very well." said Falmond. "Get your plans together and we will discuss them further at the next meeting.

15

Jori was impatient. The one moment he had been waiting almost two years for, had finally come. He had proved his worth to the council battle after battle. They even accepted his defeats and never questioned his role or standing as a leader... not since the first meeting. That said, Jori was always concerned. He was concerned about the fragility of his place in the council; he had no powers that separated him from one of his generals, and if he ever lost the backing of his men, he would lose his place immediately. What Jori failed to see was that this was his strength, his constant fighting and pushing for respect from both those below him and above him (in his eyes at least) is what made him so good at what he did. He never gave way to complacency and with Lowena keeping him in line, always carried out his actions with a measured and calculated approach.

The council met at the usual time, which was excruciating for Jori, who could not have been more eager to set his plans in motion. In his mind, they were already too late. He had spent almost every hour obsessing and deliberating over his strategy for what was surely to become the biggest success in his short, but intense military career. He had accounted for every eventuality and with Lowena's assistance, he had mitigated almost all risks that he could imagine. Thankfully, it did not take long for the council to approve his plans, and he was able to get to work.

The mission was simple, his armies would divide into small units and spread across the lands closest to the council's central base. They would fan out, spreading like a wild fire. As their reach spread, more troops would be deployed to allow for a bigger circle. Any land behind the circle was considered reclaimed, and aid could be administered safely from behind the advancing circle. No less than one quarter of all troops would remain in the council's town, so that it was not exposed at any time. If any of the troops along the front line encountered strong resistance, they would retreat half the men to the council and the other half would assist in battle. It was simple, yet complex enough to prevent risk, and it was carried out to perfection.

The circle spread out from the capital, fanning out across derelict villages, gaining aid from those who had not been invaded. Most villages that were recovered were empty, but on occasion there were slaves who were freed and returned to nearby villages to great fanfare and celebration. News spread across the land, and for the first time in what had seemed like a decade, villagers across the united lands began to feel free again. Free from fear and worry, free to go about their lives again. As were nursed back to health, reports started to come back to the council.

"The majority of villagers state that the invaders retreated somewhere between three and five days ago. They all say that they headed either east, south-east or south." Proclaimed one of the generals as he addressed the council. "None have been captured or seen since."

"That's our land." Seethed Heilmur.

"Well, steady on. I believe that during these difficult times, those are all of our lands… don't you agree?" Said Bestos, one of the scientists from the North-East, having grown significantly in confidence over the last two years. Like Millen, he was an impressively large man, with thick, short black hair, dense black stubble and arched, angular eyebrows that added a constant intensity to his expressions.

17

"Yes, of course. But those are *our* people. Those are *witches*. And we have heard nothing from them about retreating barbarian hoards, nothing even close." Heilmur was visibly angry now, and more than a little worried.

"It's possible that the communications channels have broken down in that area. We can send a team to go and investigate." Offered Bestos.

"We don't use your pathetic inventions; they are slow and untrustworthy. We use the old ways, which are not prone to collapse unlike your *technology*." Tempers had flared in the council hall before, but for cracks to be showing so visibly at such a crucial stage did not bode well. Sensing an opportunity, Jori sat forward in his seat.

"The way I see it, they are weak, they are hungry, and they have sought shelter somewhere in the witch's realm. We should go after them now and finish them once and for all. If we give them time to recover, we could lose it all." he was not going to give up on the greatest victory of his life after he had come this far. Victory was within his reach and he wasn't going to let it slip.

"What do you suggest we do then, Jori?" asked Falmond.

"We take all available troops and send them east. We have enough to attack from all sides and cover all ground. Heilmur, if your witches are in trouble in some way, we can help them, but we need enough force.". Heilmur gave a warm look to Jori, a level of warmth that a witch hardly seemed capable of showing. Thankfully, it was fleeting and went unnoticed.

"I don't think that's wise; we can't send all of our troops to one realm, it will leave us too exposed in every other area, not to mention the council." Said Millen.

"We can't be exposed; we've covered every realm and reclaimed almost every village. It's only a matter of time until all lands are returned to us, but we can't risk taking so long. Not now." Jori's voice cracked into a pleading tone that he regretted. Falmond interjected.

"You're right about one thing, we are short of time. It's clear we are divided; we should vote on this issue and move forward with whatever the council decides." The council agreed and the votes were cast.

The council still held its twelve original members. One wizard and three witches from the South-East, three scientists from the North-East, three industrialists from the North-West, Liston, a financial specialist from the mid-land and Jori from the South-West. The South-West was small, and Jori had come to see just how undeveloped it was. Its population was large, but it lacked infrastructure and any sort of modern development. The more Jori saw of the other realms, the more he was embarrassed of his own. Considering how proud Jori was of the home he had created and the accomplishments that had brought him to his seat at the council, this was a very uncomfortable feeling for him to experience. The votes were split straight down the middle, the northern votes were typically conservative and sided with caution, whereas the South favoured aggression. Lowena winced as the votes were announced. Now, more than ever, she feared for Jori. However much he needed this victory, she needed him more, and she needed him alive. Failure in the East would cost Jori more than his seat at the council, it could cost them all their lives.

Millen saw Lowena's reaction, and within it an opportunity. "So that's that… Straight down the middle. We need a casting vote. Someone with a measured, balanced approach of which we all respect. Don't you agree?" he cast his hard gaze to Lowena and it softened. "Lowena, you know the details of this particular issue as well as anyone. I know where your heart lies on the issue, but I think we can all agree that you are able to use your head when needed?". All the time Millen was addressing Lowena, he was fishing around the room for nods of approval; nods he received from all corners of the hall. He continued. "Given where my vote lay, I would suggest that my nomination would be considered fair and without bias?"

"I would agree with you there Millen, I would suggest if anything the bias lies with the opposition." Bestos' scepticism was echoed among the other Northern leaders, who were beginning to shuffle in their seats as they raised eyebrows in the direction of Millen, with hope of an explanation. Millen had to ease their doubts.

"I'm aware of Lowena's position in this matter, as are you all. I am also aware of her logic in the face of adversity and the strength she possesses in order to defy her husband if it is necessary. If I am willing to place faith in her to decide our fate, given all of this, I would hope that you would join me."

"Don't I get a say in this?" blurted Jori, his voice cracking again, this time with more despair than desperation.

"NO" replied the entire room in unison. This felt like the first thing they had agreed on in quite some time.

"So, it is agreed?" asked Bestos. The response from the room was a resounding 'yes'.

Lowena's heart sank. This wasn't what she was here for. She had agreed to leave her home two years ago so that she could support her husband. He was the reason that she was here, not the council, and not the war. But the war affected everyone; it wasn't just the concern of Jori and the council. Everyone who she had helped in her life, all the time and energy she had spent on nurturing those who needed it most, would be wasted if their efforts with the council failed. Jori had always been her main concern, but to favour him over the countless other lives that could be threatened if he was wrong, would be more devastating that one man's bruised ego. If it was a choice between siding with Jori or the rest of humanity, she knew where she would stand even though she loved him as she did.

If only it was that clear cut, she could make that decision and work on Jori afterwards if she needed to, *but Jori could be right*. If the attack in the witch's realm is successful, then all these decisions, all the risk and worry would be over. They could finally bring peace to the lands and return to their happy lives, that now seemed like a distant memory. Wouldn't that be the better way to help people? To save them entirely, to end this all, so that they too can return to their lives? It wasn't a case of mind over heart, as Millen suggested. Yes, her head was firmly on the side of caution, it did make the most sense and was the logical, considered approach, but her heart lay not only with Jori, but with the people, with *her* people. She owed them the safety and security that can only be gained by finishing this and ending the war.

"I agree with Jori and the witches." She said, as calmly as she could manage. Now more than ever, she had to appear considered and logical, as if she was making this decision with her head, and not her heart. "As are you all, I am aware of the risk that this plan brings on, but we have to act. We must finish this once and for all. Within a week this could be over and we can return to our lands, to heal the damage that this war has inflicted." The room was still and cold. Northern eyes turned to Millen; who's plan had backfired.

"So be it." he sighed. "We wanted balance, we sought out the right answer, and we will support your decision, as long as you are sure?"

"I am. I would stake my life on it." Lowena's attempts to appear resolute were successful. She tried not to look at Jori, as if this had nothing to do with him, but of course it did. She cared for the people, but she cared for Jori equally. His visible pride filled the room once again, which only made it harder for Lowena to ignore.

Plans were set in motion at once. With all the drawn-out talks of there being 'no time to waste', haste was now of paramount importance. Although the Northern districts were in reluctant support of the final mission, there was little they could do to assist. They allocated every resource they had to the Southern members, who went about enforcing their plans in an excited frenzy, swarming around the council hall frantically, every available general flying in and out to receive their orders.

5

THE MARCH EAST

The march on the East was slow by the usual standards. The more easterly troops had to wait for the reinforcements they needed to ensure their safety. Once all parties were in place, they marched further into the witch's realm. Much of the land had been covered through the wildfire attack over the last two weeks, allowing the frontline to start off more than halfway into the South-Eastern lands.

Positivity was reverberating through the troops for the first time. For two long years these men had been defending, some no more than boys. They had seen fathers, brothers and friends fall in the face of these fierce invaders. Every battle bringing the same fear of not only what would happen to them, but what they would see happen to others. This was the first time they could head into battle to attack, not defend. They were starting to understand why the invaders always seemed to have the upper hand, they wanted the fight, they relished in it. Now these heroic defenders had turned into warriors, the enemy stood no chance. They had seen them off before, and every soldier here had lived to tell the tale; they had done it before, but this time would be different. Every single warrior had lost someone to the barbarians, and while this seemed to not affect their enemies, it burned within each one of them. This potent cocktail of their newfound confidence and fiery lust for vengeance gave the people's army an air of invincibility... the barbarians stood no chance.

Usually far from battle, the witches could feel the energy reverberating throughout the army that surrounded them. Witches were not entirely unhelpful in battle, but the nature of their witchcraft added little in the frantic chaos of the frontline. Witches need quiet to work their magic, they need to be the power in the room, and the fury of battle makes this almost impossible. These witches were not sent to assist with combat, but as guides. This was their land, though they had not returned for some time. They not only knew the terrain, but the enchantments and powers of these mystic lands. They knew more than any that nothing in the East was ever as it seemed. Spells could be cast to make entire towns appear, or disappear, forests could be conjured from thin air, and mountains could be summoned from a mere pebble. They knew the land and their eyes could see what the soldiers could not, but they were also to serve as the ears of the council. As Heilmur had sharply pointed out, the witches had been communicating across vast distances for as long as anyone could recall, so having eyes and ears on the ground could prove to be the council's best chance of a successful attack.

It had been two days since the combined troops had set out. They knew this would be a long trek and they had supplies to last them weeks. They had passed empty village after empty village, without a single living soul to indicate if they were on the right path. As they approached Luola, one of the larger towns in the witch's realm, a feeling of unease swept across the five witches, who were now leading the way. "Stop." said Korvat, the oldest of the five. "This doesn't feel right. We need to tread carefully."

"With all due respect, Korvat, nothing has felt right since we left the camp. It's been too quiet for too long." Groaned Pentlow, a tall, slender general. "It doesn't take a witch to see that something's wrong. Hopefully something very wrong for these savages."

"It's magic I'm talking about. I can feel a strong presence of magic and we are getting closer."

"Of course." snarked Pentlow "Have you forgotten where we are?" he threw a warm, charming smile towards Korvat, which was snuffed out immediately by her cold, stern stare.

"Just shut up and keep your eyes peeled. I don't know what this is, but it feels wrong. All wrong."

As they ventured through the open gates of the deserted town, the witches convened and started to whisper and chant.

"Probably alerting the council." Chimed Milden, a stout, fresh-faced young General.

"Yes, I'm sure they are. But what would they report? There's nothing here!" Pentlow Replied with worry starting to creep into his otherwise smooth voice.

As the soldiers cautiously spread through the grey, lifeless town, a voice came from an alley not far from the gates.
"HERE! HERE! She's dead! I think… She's… HERE! Come here!" the soldier's confusion was understandable. The two generals arrived first and immediately knew that they were out of their depth. "Fetch the witches." Said Milden grimly.

No-one needed to call out or alert the witches. In a heartbeat, they hurried over to the woman's body, gliding swiftly through the cold, empty streets. As the five arrived, their faces fell cold and dark. Blood drained from their sharp, angular faces and their fear became visible in their trembling hands. "No man did this, this wasn't them." The witches turned to retreat, so that the council could be alerted. As they swooped off, Pentlow grabbed Korvat's arm.

"Who then?" he barked, his smooth voice replaced by fear and anger.

"Witches. Or wizards. But magic. Magic killed this woman." She slithered off to join the huddle of witches chanting and whispering back at the gate.

Pentlow didn't need to be told that magic had been the demise of this poor woman. He could see it in her face, or what was left of it. Her warped, twisted features were tightly wrapped in dark, stretched colourless skin. Her eyes hollow, black pits of nothingness. Her flesh had left her, leaving nothing but sharp deformed bones suffocated in thick, charcoal skin. The look carved on her face said it all; her death may have been quick, but it was not painless.

The soldiers picked up their pace. As the vast army spread through the abandoned city, the calls came flooding in, each one felt like a dagger to the witches.

6

TAKING RESPONSIBILITY

Word reached the council immediately and attentions turned to the high witches. "What do you make of this?" asked Bestos, trying not to sound accusatory. He knew how sensitive witches were and did not want the wrath of an angry Vahvuus directed towards him. Her power was unmatched, and he was more than aware that he had only ever seen a fraction of what she was capable of. She had always taken a silent role during discussions, only called upon when someone needed a particularly sharp word or cutting remark, yet it was clear that within the faction of mystic leaders, she was the most feared and powerful.

"It seems as though our people have turned on their own kind. I can't think why. Our bond is what gives us our strength, to weaken that is to threaten our entire existence. There must be some reason. Maybe the dead witches they found were helping the barbarians or offering them sanctuary." Heilmur tried to offer some balance to the situation, while attempting to dull the sharp blade of blame that was clearly being directed their way.

"If our witches killed in this way, it would have clearly been an act of self-defence. What your soldiers have seen in Luola is what we call 'extrusion'. It is a way of killing by extracting the victim's life source, their essence. To kill a mortal this way results in death, but to kill a witch also takes their power and that power must be handled carefully."

Jori stayed silent throughout this exchange. Having devised this plan, he was keen not to have his head anywhere near the block. He had gained the trust and support of the witches as soon as word came that the barbarians were heading East, but now his own trust had come into question. How well did he know witches? Before the days of war, he had never even thought that a witch or wizard could exist, let alone that he would meet one in person. The last two years had been a steep learning curve for Jori, but one that he took in his stride, as he always had. He had become close to several witches in his time here, none more than Heilmur, whom he hoped he could stay in contact with once the mission had been a success. He was fond of Heilmur, but bore no thoughts of romance, there was no level of warmth or softness to a witch, not even close to that required for intimacy; he really didn't know how the wizards did it. He supposed that like he had witnessed throughout his time in the council, when it came to witches, wizards just did what they were told.

Despite his fears, Jori knew that he had to stand behind the witches, as they had done for him. He was hoping that this wouldn't be necessary, that the matter could be resolved before he needed to get involved.

Millen adopted an authoritative stance, as if it would make his words more agreeable. "Whatever happened there, and whatever the motive... we need to act now. What has happened in Luola is done and we can't change that, we must carry on with our plans. We sent out our troops in search of barbarians and all they have found is a few dead witches."

"A few dead witches!?" Vahvuus screamed, the air seeming to vanish entirely from the large council hall. "Those are not a few dead witches. Those are hundreds of my people, innocently and brutally murdered. The consequences of which could have ramifications far beyond the comprehension of simple minded, knuckle-dragging trolls like you and your kind!" someone needed to intervene. Not a single drop of blood had been spilt since Jori's plans to attack had been set in motion, and it was becoming increasingly likely that the council hall would see the first. He reluctantly interjected.

"My fellow leaders. This type of conflict will not help us at all. We can't have the fate of our people dictated by the emotions of us few in this hall. We must act for the greater good. While Millen's words were ill conceived and ill advised, his point remains true. We must focus on what we do next."

"And what is that" seethed Heilmur. Jori was unaccustomed to such a harsh tone from his new friend, but was still relieved to be addressing her over Vahvuus, who was now sitting, but casting icy stares at her Northern counterparts that were felt by all present.

"We have to push on. We have to find the barbarians quickly, before any other witches get hurt." He cast his gaze at the witches in the hope that they would see his compassion for their people and soften. Whilst they acknowledged his gesture, all hopes of softening were gone. "Do you have any idea where they could be? If anyone from the East is involved, is there anywhere they could go?

"The Caves" said Henki, her voice quiet but unwavering. "They would be in the caves." Henki, the third high witch was almost always silent. The rest of the council saw this as a blessing of sorts. Henki was not fierce or powerful like Vahvuus, she was not pleasant and accommodating like Heilmur. She was troubling. She moved like a snake, slithering and writhing around in her chair, even when sitting still. There was a mesmerising, almost intoxicating quality to Henki, and one that even the simplest mortal could tell was trouble. Over the course of their time together, Henki spoke at most five times. Each time, her words were so twisted and deceptive that they left the council members unnerved and confused. No-one knew what she did when she wasn't attending meetings, she was like a ghost, never seen. To have her speak up at such a crucial time with her uneasy, unhelpful riddles would have been the last thing the council needed. But she spoke simply and truthfully.

"You're right Henki." Said Heilmur, who had calmed slightly since her stab at Jori only a moment ago. "There are caves behind Luola, we call them the 'Cooking Caves'. They house great power and if witches are involved in any way, that's where they would be."

As time passed in the council hall, the temper of the witches gradually faded. Having been so incensed at the accusations directed at their people earlier, doubt was beginning to set in. Their people were involved one way or another and there was a chance that the witches were at fault somehow. They would have to take responsibility for that, and they were beginning to know it.

7

THE FINAL PUSH

The orders from the council came swiftly. The army was not even close to finishing their sweep of the city, but they had seen enough. The bodies were all the same, the same horrifying expressions, the same hard, hollow bodies. One of those images would stay with a man for a lifetime, but the search party had become numb from so many discoveries. The orders were a welcome relief to the soldiers, who had no intention of delaying when they heard the call to retreat. The colour had gone from their faces and the song had vanished from their voices.

Thankfully, the army was large. The largest the world had ever seen. They were organised, they had the most advanced weapons ever created and save for the men who entered Luola... they were still confident. Fuelled by the vengeance that was still coursing through their veins, the army pushed on along the city outside of the city walls.

Milden was at the front of the troops with Pentlow. They were jaded and hollow from their experience in the city, but they had to lead their men, regardless. The city's walls loomed over them as they rode aside, knowing the horror of what was contained within and fearing the cause. "What *was* that?" Asked Milden.

"It must be witchcraft." Pentlow replied.

"You should ask the witches. They are the ones talking to the council, and these are their lands. Those were *their* people."

"They were. Which is why I'm not asking them."

The men rode on silently, disconnected from the buzzing excitement of the thousands of warriors surrounding them.

They arrived at the caves at dusk, halting their troops once they were in sight. "We're here." Korvat said faintly to Pentlow.

"We're here!" he bellowed to his troops, ready to prepare them for battle. As he puffed out his chest to begin his rallying speech, Korvat's hand sprung sharply around his neck.

"Not another word, you fool.", she hissed. Any hopes of camaraderie that he had thought was growing between the two of them quickly vanished. "If something is in there, we need to be careful."

"Careful? He scoffed. "Take a look lady, that there is the largest army anyone has ever seen. Those savages are hungry and scared and hiding in a cave. They are the ones who need to be careful. One word from me and they will gut that rock like a fish, quicker than you can cast one of your spells." Pentlow's confidence had usually made his life easier; combined with his good looks and slender figure, his self-assured demeanour had made him a natural leader and a persuasive man. To Korvat, it was repulsive. A symbol of everything wrong with mortal men; no abilities, no powers, but all the talk.

"We need to go in slowly, send a small group of men, and one of my witches. They can tell us what is inside and we can decide our plan from here, we can consult the council if we need to."

"OK. We'll do it your way, but night is fast approaching, and there's no way I'm setting up camp in that city."

"If the cave is clear, we can camp in there. From inside the cave, I can cast some protective spells that will keep us safe. For now, let's see if the cave is hiding anyone."

Milden wasn't the bravest general and whatever bravery he possessed had taken a serious beating inside the city walls. He was however, impatient. The thought of waiting for hours on end, next to the overbearing presence of Luola and the memories held within would be too much to bear. "I'll go." He said, with all the confidence he could manage. He took a group of fifty men (what felt like a grain of sand next to their sprawling desert of an army) and joined the witches. He set off with the witch Tuuli at his side, both trying and failing to look at ease. "So how does it work then?" he asked "...this communication thing of yours."

"You wouldn't understand, but we reach the other witches through vibrations. The further they are, the bigger the vibration needed and the more witches it takes. I should be able to talk to them quite easily on my own from this distance." Tuuli was young and quite pretty for a witch, the bright white skin on her sharp features catching the light harshly from under her hood. Milden rode on, his urge to impress the young witch buoying him enough to calm his nerves.

It had been ten minutes. "No word from Tuuli, the last message was all clear. No sign of anyone there." Korvat and Pentlow had set themselves on a large rock with a good view to the cave entrance. The three other witches were huddled behind them, ready to relay any messages to the council.

"Just how big is this cave of yours?" Pentlow's voice had returned to its usual smooth tone.

Before she had time to answer, Korvat fell to a heap, clutching her head and wailing. "GO!" She screamed, with a desperate animalistic terror in her lungs. "GO NOW!" and then her writhing body fell still and flat.

Pentlow had no idea what was happening. How could he? He was on his feet ready to give the signal but he did not know what signal to give. Attack? Retreat? Go where? He went with his gut, as he always had. "Attack!" He bellowed, holding his sword in the air as he usually did.

It was only after the vast sea of his army started flowing towards the entrance of the cave that it became clear. He was wrong.

What emerged from the cave that night had defied everything Pentlow knew to be true. He had been fortunate enough to see some of the witch's incarnations before. He was part of the team that was charged with attempting to extinguish the rampant fire caused by the fire eagles, a mission that was fruitless, but it did allow him to catch sight of the creatures several times. Whilst their existence defied all logic, they could be easily explained, they were giant eagles, with fire bursting from their shrieking beaks. The same could be said of other reports of mystic creatures; wolves, only much larger, horses with six legs, lions with the form of men, but this… this was different.

The beasts that spewed forth out of the cave bore no resemblance to any animal he had witnessed. Vomited out into their unnatural existence, they had the form of men, with two legs and arms and a head, but to say they were in any way human could not be further from the truth. Their skin was a mess of green, red, brown, and black, cracked, and hard. Spiked bone protruded from their flesh angrily, as if trying to escape the evil within. Their limbs were wide and deformed; twisting and jolting as the beasts burst forwards at pace. Their wide shoulders immediately housed their short, deformed heads. Their eyes burned yellow without a shred of humanity or even an animalistic nature… there was only rage. Their nostrils were crude holes, poked into misshapen skulls, above open angry mouths full off a jumble of fangs and teeth. Their hideous, deformed nature was a mere curiosity in comparison to their most deadly asset… their size. Five times the size of even the largest man, their arms were as thick as trees and mouths the size and shape of a roaring open fire. How these creatures could survive defied belief, but they were not created to survive… only to kill.

And kill they did. As they surged forward effortlessly through the sea of men beneath him, Pentlow was almost in awe of their power. He was one of the few who was unfortunate enough to be able to witness these creatures; all others who stood in their path did not have the time. They waded through the vast army at speed, tearing limbs, crushing bodies, and clawing flesh at they drove on. Not one man would be left to survive in their wake.

The combined army of the people had long since passed the hundreds of thousands, and while the beasts had one thousand at most, that was enough. Wave after wave of the monsters thundered out of the cave, a low groan growing into a loud roar by the time they clashed with the army. All feelings of vengeance and anger had quickly been replaced terror, bypassing the familiarity of fear. What the soldiers now felt was pure, unadulterated terror.

As Pentlow watched in abject horror, the army that he was so proud of, with all its strength and power was ripped to nothing, like soft paper. It was no fault of theirs, they were capable, they were strong, but no human could offer any resistance to what they faced that evening. Within ten minutes, the entire first wave of the army was destroyed. The ground littered with indiscriminate body parts and wet with blood and mud. As the creatures surged up the hill in front of him, their furious roars deafening as they galloped towards him, Pentlow knew that all was lost. Not just for him, not for his armies, but for all mankind.

8

WHAT MUST BE DONE

The witches on the hill behind Pentlow had managed to fulfil their role. While Korvat had lay writing on the floor, they knew what they must report. The council fell silent for a moment, having seen the life sapped from the faces of the witches at the table.

"What's happened" Millen asked, knowing that he did not want to hear the answer.

"We've lost." Heilmur replied, her voice disintegrating into almost nothing. "Something came out of the caves. Something dreadful, something magical."

"That doesn't mean we've lost!" offered Jori, half out of optimism and half hope. "Whatever it is, we have more than enough men to defend against it, and we've also got it cornered into the cave. Did they say what it was? Are the barbarians using it?"

"They aren't using it, they *are* it. The barbarians have been bewitched and they are… different."

"Different?" asked Jori, the confidence slipping from his voice.

"Yes, they are more beast than man. Bigger, stronger and more powerful than anything we have in our army." Heilmur was losing the energy to speak, she was giving in to fear and panic.

Having seen the reaction from the witches and witnessing Jori's failed attempt to propose a positive solution to the problem, Millen could sense the severity of the situation. "What does this mean?" his troubled gaze pointed towards the faltering Heilmur.

Vahvuus interjected, seeing the weakness in Heilmur. "It means that it is finished. If these creatures are as the witches say, then it would have taken an unimaginable amount of sorcery to summon them. Nothing your mortal armies and sophisticated technology can do will ever stop what is to come. They will finish our armies within no time and will be here within a day."

"What about magic then?" burst Bestos. "Your witches created the beasts; can't you create our own? Can't you fight their magic with yours? I thought you four were the most powerful sorcerers from the realm. Where is *our* monster army?"

"Three witches cannot bewitch an entire army; we simply do not have that much power. Not even us. It would take…" she paused and visibly shuddered. "It would take the power of a thousand witches to perform such a spell."

"Luola" sighed Henki.

"Yes. I fear you are right. If someone were to extrude the power from all those witches and transfer it forward, this spell it would be possible, especially from inside the cave."

"Well then what do we do?" Bellowed Bestos, growing tired with the witches' posturing and pondering "It's all good and well marvelling at the great power of your magic, but if we don't have enough of our own, then how do we fight back?"

"We can't." conceded Jori, his voice flat with the realisation that his role in this tragedy was clear, he was the main instigator. It was his fault. "We have no men to deploy, and even if we did, it doesn't sound like it would make any difference. If these barbarian creatures can get through our vast army, then there isn't a man or woman alive who could stand a chance."

"No!" Bestos boomed. "We are not going to just give up. There must be something we can do?"

The witches shared a curious look; a look no mortal at the table could decipher. Vahvuus stood up. "They are not upon us yet, and we're not going to be able to find a solution if we stand around this hall shouting at each other. I suggest we split up and try to find solutions. Jori, Lowena... come with us. You northern men can shout amongst yourselves if you feel it would aid the situation." She gave the men no time to agree and swept out of the hall in a hurry, with Heilmur sharply dragging Jori with them.

"It looks like you have a plan." Jori enquired hopefully.

"Not a plan. An idea. A hint of what could save us. The only thing that is left at this point." Heilmur had sparked back into life, the defeat had vanished from her voice, there was even a touch of hope. "What the Northerner said. He wasn't wrong. There is something we can do, even with only our magic."

"Well let's do it then!" Jori was rejuvenated. At this stage any glimmer of hope was like the blinding mid-day sun to him. If all was not lost, he had not failed yet.

"It's not as simple as that. It's a powerful and unpredictable spell. There's no telling what could happen, and…" Heilmur paused, to allow Jori to feel the gravity of what was to come "It will require great sacrifice."

"Oh, I see. Well, that's understandable I suppose, given what I've learned so far about your ways. What kind of sacrifice? And from whom?"

"From *all* of us. It will take all three of us to sacrifice our essence, in order to summon something powerful enough to help. This will destroy us. Falmond can finish the spell, and speak for us at the council, but it will mean the end of us three."

"Oh." Said Jori, trying to look as sincere as possible. He had only known the witches for a couple of years, and two of them not very well, if at all. His friendship with Heilmur would be greatly missed, but on balance, it could have been a lot worse. If this works, he can go back to his life, the same life he had before he knew of the existence of witches at all. "I am sorry, are you sure there is no other way?"

"No, this is what must be done. We must be responsible for our decisions in the council and the actions of our people in the realm. We must *all* take responsibility Jori. That's why we are here."

"Well, I suppose you are right. We are responsible for the future of humanity, and that is no easy burden. Losing the three of you would be a huge loss to us all, and one that will stay with me until my last day." Jori's honest attempt at sincerity was bordering on the melodramatic now, but he stopped himself before he went too far.

"Jori…" Heilmur purred, softening her voice to a point where he hardly recognised it. "When I said we must make a great sacrifice, I meant from us all."

"Oh." Jori pulled back slightly and adjusted his sympathetic, almost cowering stance. "What do you mean? From who? From me? I suppose it only fair. I shouldn't expect you to lay down your lives for the sake of humanity and stand idly by. What is it that you need?" He had puffed out his chest and was standing proud behind his strong, noble words.

"We need you to make the biggest sacrifice of all Jori, but it is not your life that we need."

"No! What? No! What do you mean? No." Jori had caught the eyes of the other two witches. Eyes that were cast firmly towards Lowena. Lowena had been silent throughout this strange and uncomfortable discussion. The weight of the tragedy they faced weighed heavily on her, as did her part in it. She knew better, of course she did. She had gone against her better judgement twice, directly leading them all to this situation. She stood by her husband as he would expect, but at what cost? She claimed to love and care for the people, for *all* her people. But she knew that her decision was selfish, for her own relationship with her husband, for one man in an increasingly large world. If Lowena had not been given the casting vote, perhaps she would not take such responsibility. But she had. She hadn't even tried to refuse, she had taken the opportunity, flattered by the esteem the council had granted her and a victim of her own ego. Who was she to decide the fate of so many, and for what reason? She was merely the wife of a farmer, arrogantly aiding others to fuel her own self-worth. She was no better than any of them, if anything she was worse.

Lowena was spiralling in a whirlwind of self-doubt. her intentions were good, she knew this, somewhere, but all things she knew were uprooted in her mind; circling and spinning until she could barely see.

As she felt the presence of the witches' gaze, calm was restored to her dizzy mind. She had heard what they had said, and she had felt what it meant. She knew what needed to be done.

"We need to summon a creature, as our people in the cave have done. We have no cave, and we have but three witches, so we will not be able to spare the source of the creature." Heilmur had become sterner and more resolute. Her words carrying the promise of success, as if to mask the severity of the consequences.

"Well use me then, use my 'source' to make your beast. I am strong, I can fight, my beast would be far deadlier than my gentle wife's creation. I've told you I'm willing to sacrifice it all, and I am!" Jori was still in his proud stance, but his tone now held more anger than pride.

"That's the point Jori. Casting a spell like this needs balance as you know... all spells do. Creating a monster from a strong, powerful man would create a weak and fearful creature, and that is not what we need is it?"

"Well, no. But there must be something different we can try. Anything but this?"

"This is it Jori, it's all we have and even then, it might not work. It's not just our best chance, it's our only chance."

"But why Her? Why my Lowena? You're telling me that in this whole city there is no one else suitable?"

"You know why. There is no one *more* suitable. We must be certain of the source's character for this to work.

Otherwise, it's too much of a risk. We know Lowena well enough for the spell to be cast."

"Well, she won't do it. You'll have to find someone else."

"Yes, I will." Lowena's tone was calm and composed. If anything, she was a little relieved when the witches turned to her. In all this frantic fighting and with the end of their lives much closer than they had ever expected, this sacrifice offered Lowena a way out, on her terms. Her troubled mind was offered a way out of doubt and introspection. Even if there were another way, the slaughter of all those men lay on her shoulders. She would have to live with that until her death. Bringing that day forward would only lessen the long suffering that she was due for many years to come. To die knowing that her sacrifice was pure and that her intentions were unquestionable would give her peace in whatever lay waiting for her after this life. Peace that she would not otherwise be entitled to.

She knew that a circle of witches was no place for an emotional conversation between husband and wife; their icy cold presence and emotional indifference could suck the feeling out of any room. She pulled Jori aside, his reluctance to move with her a clear indication of his position on the matter. "Jori, this is happening. The witches need me. Everyone needs me. This is what I was brought here for, this is my purpose."

"I brought you here. To help me. How is you sacrificing yourself going to help me?" Jori was never particularly interested in the higher thoughts that life can offer. Lowena ruminated endlessly on the powers above them, posturing poetically about the endless possibilities of life beyond their mortality. Jori did no such thing. He knew what he could see and that to him, was all there was. Their introduction to magic when they joined their fellow councillors showed this stark contrast.

While Lowena was immediately drawn to the mystical theology that she and the wizards discussed often, Jori was only interested in its practical application. Lowena could tell that she had lost Jori when she brought in the philosophical argument, and she needed to speak to him on his terms. She had convinced him of many things in the past and often managed to persuade him softly and gently over an evening into seeing how there may be another way of thinking about an issue. This was not one of those times. Time, it felt, had never been scarcer or of more significance than in this exact moment. If they were to change their fates, they must do so now.

"Jori, this is happening. I know that you don't want to lose me… of course you don't. But you will. One way or another, this is it. If I cannot do this for our people… for you… then I will no longer be able to stand by your side. You either lose me to this cause… to *your* cause, or you lose me anyway. Let me do this. Please."

"I need time to think."

"There is no time. You know that. All there is, is what is happening now. And I'm sorry Jori, but it is happening."

Peering back at the group of witches, it was clear that the privacy they were looking for was not possible. Hopeful, expectant eyes shone back at them through the shadowy cloaks of the witches. Falmond was looking back more knowingly, reassuring Lowena with his soft eyes, peering out through his bushy eyebrows.

"We need to tell the council." Heilmur tried to hide her excitement, which wasn't easy for a witch, as it was an emotion that they rarely felt.

In the council hall, the northern men were waiting. They had stayed where they were since the southern leaders had departed, having said all they had to in the previous meeting. During their absence, the men could only fret, and as a result were anxiously pacing around the council hall, like giant chess pieces awkwardly controlled by an external force. "Well…?" Millen blurted at once. It was clear that their time had been spent debating what the witches would devise, rather than devising suggestions of their own.

"We have an idea, but it will take great pain, great sacrifice…. And quiet." From the look Vahvuus was giving the other councillors, it's clear what she meant. They began their exit.

"What are you going to do?" asked Bestos.

"We are going to summon a beast. One creature with enough power to destroy the barbarian monsters."

"What kind of creature?" curiosity and slight excitement had crept into Bestos' shallow voice.

"We don't know yet. The source dictates the creature, like a light shining against a mirror."

Bestos and the other men had no idea that could have meant, but a plan was more than they had provided, and at this stage it was the only hope they had left.

"Good." He said solemnly "The word from your witches is that our army is finished."

9

SACRIFICE

Jori's involvement in what was to come was frustratingly limited. Much as Lowena had been when she sat through endless council meetings, Jori was present but powerless. Sitting anxiously alongside Falmond in the seats usually occupied by the assistants to the council, he had never felt so insignificant. To all intents and purposes, at this stage… he was.

Jori had not given his blessing for this to happen, but he had not stopped it. He could not have stopped it. This was Lowena's choice, but not one she made alone and Jori knew this all too well. His time on the side-lines made him think, and he had a lot to think about. What if he had not pushed for the march East? Would they still be in this position? He reassured himself with the thought that whatever had come out of those cursed caves would have emerged anyway. But they wouldn't have had their entire army waiting outside, offered up on a plate. They wouldn't have been left defenceless against what was sure to be a gruesome attack from the creatures. Maybe they would? Maybe this was all destined to be, and whatever Jori (or anyone else for that matter) decided within these walls made little to no difference at all. He was beginning to think like Lowena. He could see the appeal; it was a comforting notion. If nothing he did ultimately made a difference, then he wasn't really to blame for any of it. He basked in the relief that the notion brought over him, bathing briefly in the warmth of his exoneration.

His comfort was unfortunately brief. As the witches chanted and circled around his wife, Jori became painfully aware that he was an outsider. Not because he wasn't involved in the summoning ritual, or that he was instructed to stay silent as if he were a child, but because they were all freeing themselves. Everyone in that room had been complicit in causing the death of hundreds of thousands of men; and in doing so threatened the entire existence of the four realms. By making their sacrifices, these four women were allowing themselves peace and granting their own redemption. It felt odd to Jori, to watch on, enviously as these women give up their lives, like an outsider at a party he was not invited to. His jealousy was misplaced, he thought. If anything, *he* was making the greater sacrifice, *he* would have to life with all of this and *they* were taking an easier path.

As the chanting went on, Jori began to grow impatient, knowing what was to be the outcome of this ritual made the wait excruciating. But then, as the chanting stopped, the room swelled with tension, and the walls vibrated with anticipation. The floor began to crack and warp and the witches fell to their knees. In the circle they had made around Lowena's flat, tense body, clouds of colour started to appear.

Wisps of purple, blue and black began to spiral together from each of the witches, like steam from three boiling pots. As the cloud grew, it spun faster and faster until it formed a swirling vortex of energy above Lowena as she cowered beneath, trying to stay still.

The Vortex spiralled tighter, sucking in the air from the room as it twirled. With one sharp stab, the cloud darted down into Lowena. As it entered her body, the witches fell back silently, their hard, hollow bodies falling to the floor like wooden blocks. The room started to shake. Jori was paralysed with fear and dread. His wife, consumed by powerful forces about to steal from him what held most dear.

Despite the fear, the panic and the confusion, Jori could still see his love, diligently trying to play her part as well as she could. There had been an air of determination etched firmly onto her face throughout the chanting and spinning, but now there was calm. Half from fear, Lowena had kept her eyes closed tightly for the duration of the spell, had she seen the power of what was swirling above her it could have broken her resolve. But now her eyes were closed, but not tightly. She knew that whatever was about to emerge from within her would change their fates and end what they had started. She had done it.

As the ground shook and the walls began to collapse, Jori could only stare open mouthed as he saw the monster emerge. What started as a dark blue cloud spiralling from her chest, flashing, and flickering like a storm, stretched to a long thin coil, twisting and writhing. It had started to take form.

Its slender body flexed and flowed underneath its midnight blue scales, rippling, and contorting as if its skin was struggling to contain the power within. Cracking through the scaly skin, two spiked wings stretched out in search of life. At the top of its body rose three fearsome heads. Snapping and hissing, retching, and roaring; the creature had been given its life. In her last living moment, Lowena opened her eyes to marvel upon the saviour she had delivered. The look of terror and agony would be carved into her face for eternity.

Jori did not have time to linger on the expression of his now deceased wife. With the witches gone, along with Lowena, he was now face to face with this hideous abomination. His attention turned to Falmond, desperately seeking guidance and reassurance.

Falmond was always slow, he never moved faster than an amble, never spoke with more than a hushed, gentle, contemplative tone. With Jori's helpless, fearful gaze cast upon him, Falmond's time to speak and act with haste and precision had come. Passing up on this opportunity, he slowly turned to Jori, raising his dark grey, overgrown eyebrows to reveal his solemn, apologetic eyes. "Well...". His delivery was agonising.

"Well, what? We do we do now?" Jori was bursting under the pressure of the situation. The great beast looming over them both, too terrified to look up at it, Jori kept all his attention on Falmond.

"Well, *we* don't do anything". Said Falmond eventually. Jori had never realised quite how irritating wizards could be. Having spent his time with witches, while Lowena had somehow enjoyed the company of these ineffective fossils. Every movement was like watching a tree grow its branches. Now here he was, at a time of great consequence and urgency, having to extract the slowly moving sap of information from the only source that could enlighten him.

"What do you mean?" The adrenaline coursing through his veins had found a useful outlet. "We can't just do nothing, there's a thirty-foot, three-headed snake slithering around the room. Or haven't you noticed that? You incompetent old goat!"

"Of course, I have Jori, I was merely saying that there is nothing I can do about this creature. It is not a matter of we, but *you*. Do you not think that this was part of our plan? What good is a powerful beast like this, without someone to command it?"

"Great, the wizard once again unable to help. Are you trying to tell me that I have to control this... this *thing*?"

"Yes. Although control may be an unwise choice of words. The bond shared between you and the source..." Noticing the anger flare beneath Jori's eyes, he corrected himself "The bond that you shared with Lowena makes this *thing* linked to you, and you to it. If you connect with it, it should follow your command."

"Should. Well, that's reassuring, thank you. Do you have any other vague insight that you would like to drip feed me?"

Jori's tirade was cut short. He could have carried on for several more minutes, but in the time the conversation had already taken, the serpent had turned its attentions towards the two men. Jori's focus on Falmond had allowed him in some way, to put the creature's presence out of his mind. But as he began to lay into the old wizard, he could feel its hot breath upon him, suffocating him with its putrid heat.

Falmond took his leave, showing as much haste as he was capable of.

Jori reluctantly turned to address the beast, who had positioned the middle of its three heads directly behind Jori. The scales of the snake's body were pitch black, except for an incandescent blue reflection. This gave the slithering nature of the snake's movement an almost seductive quality. As Jori was now face to face with the enormous middle head, he could see the soulless fury in its eyes. Around its neck, the blue tinge of the scaly body was instead a sickening yellow. Its head was slim and slender. Its breath was pure death, steaming out of its flat nostrils. Its eyes were small and shallow, thin, evil jewels shining from deep within. He cast his gaze left and right to acknowledge the presence of the other heads, and to escape the intensity of the yellow headed stare.

To the left, was the largest of the three heads, sharp, jagged scales burned red and purple, transforming into giant spiked horns at the top of its skull. Its ruby eyes burned with anger, wide and ferocious. Beyond the anger and power of this vicious head lay a mesmerising beauty. The deep red and purple scales shimmered and swirled gracefully as if to distract from the terror that it was capable of inflicting. Further away, the third and largest head stared cautiously from a distance. The emerald green head was almost twice the size of the other two, its giant, heaving jaws burying its small, deceptive eyes.

10

TAKING COMMAND

Surrounded and suffocated by these three enormous monsters, six eyes locked on to him with menacing expectation. Jori was lost. He knew that he must take hold of the situation, to command this abomination and lead them all to victory, but he just felt lost. How could he take charge at this time, he had just lost everything he held dear and the only directions he was given were the slow, pondering riddles of a useless old man. He stared blankly at the serpent, spreading his gaze across all six eyes, not trusting either head to go unwatched. His mouth was open, awaiting instruction... as was the snake.

This was no prophecy, there was no plan for what was to happen next. This was a scheme, hastily conceived in an emergency; the architects of which, were no longer alive to see it through. The more Jori chewed over this thought, the angrier he became. Anger was a common feeling for Jori, it sparked his drive and determination and maintained his air of authority. It often got him into trouble, but thanks to Lowena, it had never gone unchecked for long.

The familiarity of this anger brought comfort to Jori. Rudderless and alone, his growing rage at least had put some wind behind his sails. Fuelled by this, Jori rose from his chair and stood tall, addressing the giant serpent. Jori had never found it difficult to stand tall among his generals. He was a short, stout man with a particularly unathletic build; a stark contrast to the generals and captains that he delivered orders to. When he couldn't rely on a horse for elevation, Jori had always managed to conduct himself in a way that belied his small stature, a skill that he had found great use for in this critical moment. Legs apart, chest out, Jori stared fearlessly at the beast.

"Right..." he thundered, using the loudest, most authoritative voice he could summon, despite the creature only being a foot from his own face. "We have a job to do. A thousand barbarian monsters are marching on these lands and we need to defend them. There is only one of you, and they will be here soon, so we need to act fast." On addressing the snake, Jori had inadvertently made himself aware of the magnitude of the task they faced. Doubt began to set it, and this was not the time for it. "There may be thousands of them, but they are nothing compared to you." He reassured the snake, although as he looked further into its eyes, he knew that it needed no reassurance at all, unlike Jori. After reassuring himself with his own words, he continued. "The monsters are coming from the east. They are strong, fast and they are deadly. You need to stop them marching forwards and kill them all. Is that understood?" all three heads stared back at him. Their stares were not blank, nor empty, as their eyes were constantly burning with hatred, but they showed no signs of comprehension.

Jori thought himself a fool for believing the wizard. How could a creature like this, summoned from nothing so recently, understand the commands he was administering, as if they were trained army generals. The uneasy silence that followed Jori's futile orders lasted for a long and tense minute. Unsure what to do next, Jori turned, as if to march towards the exit.

The creature turned with him.

It is *linked* to me. Jori thought, remembering the wizard's words. The man and beast were facing the same way, towards the large, ornate doorway leading out of the large council hall. Jori puffed out his chest once again and confidently strode towards the door. As he opened it and marched through, the serpent burst through the long wall of the hall beside him, leaving the building half in ruins.

Outside the hall, stood the six northern councillors, mouths open. Jori's confidence had carried him this far. "Well… I suppose after today we won't have use for the hall… one way or another." Jori's humour had often been a useful tool for him to call upon, easing the concerns of those around him, and cutting through tense and difficult situations. The men said nothing. This was the first they had seen of the beast. Falmond had briefed them on it after his exit from the hall moments before, but nothing could prepare them for what stood before them now. Their cold, hard terror was plain for Jori to see. These usually brash and fearless men now cowered before the presence of the serpent. Jori felt a surge of pride wash over him; all this power was his to command. This creature that they feared so obviously would obey *his* command.

Turning to marvel upon his newfound ally, Jori's breath disappeared from his body. Within the walls of the large council hall, he had not been able to see the true scale of this terrifying creature. Now, in the freedom of the outside world, the snake had uncoiled and was towering above the wreckage of the hall. Its wings held the three heads high above the eight tiny men below, each one far larger than Jori had realised. Jori's pride had been replaced again by fear, and doubt had begun to creep back in. The northern eyes were fixed on Jori, cold and hopeless. Having brought him this far, his confidence could not desert him now; although he felt no amount of it, he knew how to act.

He adopted his usual stance, like a cockerel ready to crow. "I will need the council guards and a good horse. We will ride east to attack these beasts and end this once and for all." The familiarity of these words stung him. It was only a matter of days since he last said something similar, but the world was a drastically different place now. Where there was once confidence and excitement shared with the witches and his beloved Lowena, there is only despair and desperation, overshadowed and overpowered by this hideous, terrifying abomination.

11

RECKONING

There had been no time to plan, no more votes, no more discussions. The council as they knew it was no more. No one knew what could come next. Jori rode out immediately, accompanied by no more than fifty council guards on horseback; the last of the able men. Tasked with protecting the council from any surprise attacks, these men had not seen a glimpse of battle since the realms had come together.

Among the combined armies, they were the laughingstock. While the other troops earned their status as warriors and paid a heavy price in return, these capable and formidable fighters charged with endless days of standing and waiting. Now the hour was upon them, they were tasked with a challenge that no other soldier had been able to overcome; survive an encounter with the barbarian monsters.

Of course, they were not alone, to send fifty men to fight the hoard would be something much more certain than suicide. As they rode in formation behind their leader, the great snake slithered at speed alongside them. It moved with such grace that it looked like a snail's pace compared to what it was capable of. Its wings were tucked flat along its body as it swayed slowly from side to side like a gently flowing river; in contrast, the guard's horses were riding flat out to keep pace. The rate that the hoards were reported to be travelling gave them two days until their forces met, by Jori's estimations at least. There was nothing Jori could say to steady the nerves of his fresh new troops of soldiers. All the security that they needed was sliding along beside them, leaving vast trenches in its wake.

It was the evening of the second night that Jori and the guards first spotted the light on the horizon.

"Ok men, this is it. Your task in this war is simple, protect your commander. This beast obeys my command, so if I die, so do our hopes. Stay close, and hopefully we can make it out alive." Jori's words fell flat on the soldiers, accepting his orders like scorned children. Even in the most uncertain battles, orders were met with cheers of validation, as if by doing so their chances were to increase. Everyone had to believe that victory was possible. Perhaps it was their lack of battle experience, perhaps the task of protection rather than battle was not such a powerful motivation. More than likely it was the task ahead of them.

A thin line of fire and smoke traced the edge of the horizon. As Jori was administering his brief rallying speech, the line had turned thicker. Within no time, the line was now a sea of flames and dust, surging towards them with unrelenting, inescapable dread.

Jori had taken position in front of the men on top of a large pointed hill, a position that had recently bought

Pentlow an ultimately futile sliver of additional time. From here, he could see the hoard flowing down from the horizon into the valley between them. As with everyone who came before him, Jori had no experience of battle when commanding a mystical snake, how could he?

Through their surprisingly brief travels towards the battle, Jori had felt his bond with the serpent grow. At it moved alongside him, he could feel its intentions and tried to match them with his own. He could feel each movement the snake made, and practiced shaping them to his will. By the time they reached the valley, he felt more confident in his ability to control and command the creature, although a separate entity with its own mind, the snake felt like part of him.

Standing at the apex of the hill, Jori commanded the snake forward, pointing his sword high and true in front of him. This act served much more of a dramatic purpose than a practical one, and it was a pose that Jori maintained unknowingly throughout what was to come.

Until now, the guardsmen had only seen the snake at a relative canter, weaving mesmerizingly from side to side. Obeying Jori's forceful command, it was now almost straight, allowing them to see the full length of its giant powerful body. As it reached the furthest depth of the valley, the tip of its tail was still only just embarking into battle. The serpent undulated left and right, the earth beneath turning to hills and valleys behind it, carving a dry river bed deep into the ground.

As it approached the seemingly endless wave of barbarians, it stretched out its giant wings, lifting itself high in the air above them. The red headed mouth opened wide, a single, broad jet of purple and red flames bursting out, spreading itself far across the front line. The barbarians caught in the jet were turned to coal on impact, and those in any way near were caught in the inextinguishable fire it left in its path. If Jori had been aware of the true power that the snakes possessed, he would have probably commanded it to do this.

The fiery river now keeping the monsters from progressing any further, their undivided attention now firmly lay with the snake. It crashed back down into the heart of the lake of giant bodies, writhing and weaving, crushing bodies beneath its large, sharp scales.

Rising again, but lacking momentum, the middle head attacked. Twisting its head sharply, bright yellow poison spewed out from the front of two clean, long, sharp fangs. The ground beneath sizzled, the barbarian flesh melted like butter, leaving fields of scattered bones in a soup of soulless fluid. Within two swift attacks, the snake had already significantly depleted the invading forces. As it landed from the poisonous onslaught, the serpent burrowed into the ground, retreating along the valley away from the barbarian monsters. Nervous glances darted towards Jori, who was still sitting on his horse, his sword proudly in the air.

He lowered his sword. He could feel the eyes of his men digging into him. During the brief yet devastating downpour of both of fire and poison, Jori had gladly accepted the success as his own doing, despite being wholly unaware that this barrage was even a possibility. Now, he was sitting, eyes cast firmly on the snake, avoiding the eyes of his increasingly inquisitive men.

Jori could only watch as the serpent burrowed further up the valley leaving the deformed army to chase behind it. With one rapid movement, it pulled up into the air and coiled back on itself, charging back towards the battle with increased fury and faster pace. Its wings tightly contained along its body, the green head lifted and opened its enormous jaws. As it ploughed through the swirling lake of bodies, it crunched and snapped, dismembering and destroying all who lay in its path. The powerful jaws crushed through rock, ground, and barbarian alike, leaving nothing left intact but a bloody trail of rubble and bone.

And so, it went. One wave after another. One… two… three. All heads working in unison in a barrage of unrelenting attacks. Fire, poison, and power wreaking havoc on what was once a fearsome and dreadful army. Pools of liquid flesh, piles of ash and scatterings of hideous body parts littered a scarred and deformed valley.

Jori watched on, his redemption finally upon him. All the mistakes, all his sacrifices, laid to rest in the wake of this terrible creature. Their fates had been saved and their futures secured. If his mind was not so completely consumed by vengeance upon the barbarian invaders, he would have spared a thought for his love Lowena. Her ultimate sacrifice bringing into existence the salvation of the combined lands.

Not now. This was Jori's moment.

His face was illuminated with the red and purple fire of the battle ground, shining with the yellow spurts of poison in the air below them. His eyes burned with vindication as he basked in the power that he had come to possess. For Jori, at this moment, nothing was impossible. What he had witnessed within the last day had defied every belief that he had held and cost him all that he loved, in return he was granted ultimate power.

The look in Jori's eyes had not been lost on his guards. To them, he had lost control. Their calls for him to stop the beast were ignored, as it tore through every living thing in front of it. Several of the men approached Jori, to seek guidance, or to reason with him. Each time, they were cast back with a fiery stare, full of hate and fuelled by power. Whatever fear they felt towards the invading army, paled in comparison to the terror they felt upon seeing what this creature was capable of. Having stood witness to the devastation that the serpent could inflict, the men agreed that Jori was now too powerful, too consumed by the supremacy that he now possessed. As he stared, wide eyed, cackling at the desolation that lay before him, they hatched a plan. "We have to do something. He won't listen to us, just look him."

"But the snake, if we go for him, it will defend him and kill us."

"No, if he lives, the snake will surely come after us."

"I fear that it will come for us either way. It's not going to stop once this is done."

"You've seen the bond they have. If we kill Jori, the serpent will surely die. It's our only hope."

The men solemnly nodded in agreement and word spread through the ranks.

12

COMEUPPANCE

The fire below was so intense that Jori could feel it warm his face. He sat, bathing in the glow of death, comforted by his newfound retribution. Thoughts of Lowena, of sacrifice, of all those men who he had forsaken had disappeared from his mind, replaced only by the warmth and sanctuary of his newly acquired power. Glimpses of opportunity and possibility flashed past him, as he thought of an exciting new world yet to come with him at the centre, and the serpent by his side. Nothing would stop them. Nothing could stop *him*.

Jori's time in the sun was about to come to an end. The fifty soldiers who had retreated from Jori's position at the top of the hill had begun to edge closer back to him. They knew that they had to catch him by surprise so that they wouldn't attract the attention of the serpent as it swept across the valley, leaving no trace of life behind. They moved slowly on foot, using the thunderous crashes and dreadful screams of the snake to hide the sound of their shuffling, crunching armour. Not one of the fifty men dared to speak; one wrong move could threaten the lives of them all. The sheer number of guards made their task extremely difficult, but they had agreed that it would be safer to attack as a unit, rather than send one guard. The soldiers were equipped for battle, with armour, swords, and axes; they had no subtle option. If Jori caught sight of a single guard approaching with his weapon drawn, he would be able to stand a chance of survival; against all of them, he stood no chance.

Edging imperceptibly closer, the guards were almost behind him. As they drew closer, their nerves were calmed. They could see the euphoria slapped plainly across his face. The joy the serpent felt in wreaking its devastation in the valley below was shared by Jori, sat comfortably on his static horse, his eyes glowing and his smile broad. He was utterly oblivious to his surroundings. The threat had vanished from Jori's mind as soon as the serpent struck its third powerful attack. There was no way that he could have known of the new danger behind him, edging closer with painful trepidation.

With Jori blissfully unaware and consumed by his vengeance, the guards time had come. The ten men at the front of the close huddle drew their swords and began to circle behind him. They took one step closer to striking distance and his horse jerked forward. Jori was jolted out of his trance-like state and he turned to see the guards. It only took a second for Jori to realise what was happening. A cluster of guards upon him, weapons drawn, the startled, yet determined look on their faces. They had come for blood.

The guards lunged towards his horse, who thrust forwards again and carried Jori to safety. The guards ran after him, all hopes of stealth and subtlety had vanished. This was time for a full-fledged attack. Jori's horseback advantage was short lived. Just down from the smooth hill that Jori was watching from, the ground began to get softer, the mud became deeper. His horse struggled through the thick mud and the men behind surged on; clambering over each other with a vicious rage; it was his life or theirs.

Talek, his horse, ran slower and slower, barely managing a walk. He had been staring obediently into the carnage below, a mess of bright colours. In the absence of context, his mind was as usual, still. This allowed him the awareness to detect the men behind him, even if they were almost within touching distance when he did. Now, after making his escape, he was stuck. He could only watch on as his master deserted him, fleeing forward desperately on foot. Talek was not with Jori often, but he had been with him for a long time. Whilst he was rarely ridden, his time transporting Jori was an easy one. Trotting gently from grand hall to refreshments, or leisurely outrides to allow Jori to clear his head; as much as a horse could, he had enjoyed his time. He was well looked after, treated with kindness and his master was small. Now, knee deep in mud, he could only look on as his master floundered in front of him; as he turned to face his treacherous attackers, he heard their thunderous steps approach behind him.

How quickly reality had hit Jori. A mere moment ago, he was basking in his triumphant glory, his day of redemption so suddenly upon him. Now, he was on his back, clambering for his sword as the baying mob of his own men called for his blood. Fifty muddied faces, crying out for their first battle; their first victory. It would be a swift victory. In truth, Jori would struggle to best one of these trained guards. His attempts to draw his sword from the mud were certainly futile against fifty.

As he hopelessly and unsuccessfully scrambled to his feet, he looked helplessly at the faces of his attackers. They shone bright, not with anger, but with hope. At was at this point; looking up, his back in the mud, that Jori realised why. He was lost. Is this what he would become without Lowena? Such a dangerous threat that his own men would turn on him so quickly? Even in the face of certain victory? Thanks to the thick mud, their charge towards him was slow enough for Jori to resign himself to his fate. It didn't take him long to not only understand their new cause, but to agree with it. The realms could not have such unbridled power roaming free, and he had proven almost instantly that he was not worthy of such a responsibility. He stopped grasping for his wet sword, stuck deep in the mud. He stopped scrambling to find his footing to meet his new foes. He sank back, defeated, and accepted his end; *it is the right thing,* he thought. The distant battlefield made their pale, tired faces glow yellow… then purple.

Towering above the defeated man, the serpent held it's held high and focussed on the guards. Slow, steady flaps of its giant wings kept it hovering over them, assessing its prey. Before Jori had time to shift his gaze, a red and purple waterfall came flowing down in front of him. The fire was so strong and so intense that Jori was spared the agonising screams. There was no need for the serpent to administer another attack; with one burst, they were all gone. The ground beneath them hard and scorched, their bones reduced to dust. It had been so quick that Jori could not react. Any claims of 'control' or 'command' over this creature seemed foolish to him now.

He lay back into the mud unable to move, the smell and heat in front of him unbearable. The serpent gradually descended, with a gentle, sweeping grace. Aware of the snake's presence, but unable to address it, Jori lay as lifeless as the fifty men before him.

13

FROM THE ASHES

It was quite some time before he could summon the energy to move, or the courage to confront the beast. His time in the mud had taught him the consequence not only of his new power, but his life beyond Lowena. If this is what Jori would become without Lowena after one single day, then those men were right. They should not have died. Jori had wallowed in the bog of self-pity for long enough to see that their blood did not stain the conscience of the serpent, even if it had one. Their fate was his to decide and even though he did so unknowingly, the bond he shared with the creature put the guilt of their death firmly on his shoulders.

As dawn began to break, Jori knew that there was no turning back; nothing that had happened in the last few frantic days could be reversed. He could not bring back the armies that he had sent to certain death, he would not be reunited with his Lowena. The witch's lives were as irretrievable as the men who lay before him, now fading lumps of coal. He had held no power over what had come before, but comforted himself with that feeling of inevitability that had graced him once before in the council hall on the eve of Lowena's sacrifice.

All that Jori could do was shape the future. Hundreds of thousands of lives had been lost, but they would not be not in vain. The future they fought to protect was now safe. While he may have had a part in their death, he had a leading role in their ultimate victory. As the sun rose over the eastern hill where the barbarians had appeared the previous evening, Jori's aguish had turned to hope. Thoughts of his triumphant return flashed through his mind and filled his heart with pride. Finally, with the mud set hard around him, Jori broke out and rose to his feet. The serpent was waiting for him.

Jori had lay all night in that spot. Close enough to see the petrified remains of the men, like statues erected in honour of his shame; his beloved horse Talek, a monument to his betrayal. Nothing could make Jori more aware of what he had done, he would not hide from his guilt, not this time. Whatever he would do next would be in honour of the great sacrifices that had been made in these most difficult times.

Jori's journey back west was a significantly slower one than their march east the previous day. He had managed to corral one of the guard's horses, who had scattered across the valley since they were abandoned for the silent attack. Looking back at the valley for the first time in daylight, he could see the true nature of the devastation that the snake had inflicted. Giant trenches and hills were carved into the soft hills. Fire pits and poison ponds lay scattered among the remains of the barbarian invaders. Further up the hill, the site of Jori's ultimate disgrace; a small field of charcoal guards, frozen in time, their intentions laid bare for all to see. With a nod to the serpent in the direction of the muddy field, Jori set off. The ground behind him ploughed and distorted by his fearsome new ally.

14

VICTORY

The last few days in the council had been the most confusing and frustrating that any of the Northern men had encountered. Since they had reluctantly agreed to send their armies east, the rest of what was to come felt like a dream, a terrible nightmare of which they had no control. Until this point, their wise council and cunning innovation had been of great benefit to the war effort. As soon as those monsters emerged from that cave, they knew their insight and abilities were redundant. From that point forward, the Northern councillors could only act as moral advisors, although even this area became so grey that it was a near impossible task.

They sat... and they waited, inside the council hall... in silence. For men with so much to share, so much common ground, they struggled to find a single word. These were men of great power and great status. Their appointment into the council had only elevated their esteem and buoyed their self-assurance. Now, huddled together solemnly, they understood their true power, or lack of. While an uneducated farmer led a mystic serpent to battle, they helped clear the rubble in the council hall, along with the maids and cleaning staff. These proud, strong masters of industry reduced to keeping busy to try to pass time, powerless over their own futures.

At breakfast on the third day, Millen broke down. "What has happened? Surely there must be a way of telling? No reports? No witches? Nothing?"

"Now, listen Millen… this is hard for all of us. None of us know what's happening out there, but we have to keep our heads up." Said Bestos.

"Keep our heads up? For what? For all we know, we could die today. Or tomorrow. And we're keeping house like scullery maids?"

"What would you have us do? Go and join them? Return home defeated?"

"Something. Anything but this. Anything but wait for death like cowards."

"You've heard of what's out there, this isn't cowardice. What you would see as bravery would only be suicide."

"And you think it's brave, do you? What we're doing? Hiding here in the hopes that the victory is won on our behalf?"

"We have no other choice; this is not something that we can participate in. Our time will come in rebuilding once this is all over."

"And if that doesn't happen? What if this doesn't work? And how could it? One snake and fifty men against thousands?"

"You saw that thing. I don't like the chances of anything that comes up against it, monster or not."

"Yes, I saw it. I've thought of nothing else for the past two days. I can feel its eyes staring into my soul. Even if it is victorious... then what? We have that *thing* roaming the lands, destroying our halls. What will it eat... us?"

"Let's just deal with the task at hand, shall we? We'll discuss that with Jori when he returns."

"Ha... More like *if* he returns."

"The way I see it... is that no news is good news. It's been two days, and the invaders should be with us today. So, I suppose we'll find out who is right."

The discussion raged on for the rest of the day. Whether would be successful, and how many men it would take to kill a creature like that. The arguments were relentless and sometimes fierce, but they served as a welcome distraction to the silent, sombre tension that had plagued their days before.

By the time Jori had made his triumphant return, the northern men's heads were full of conflict and confusion. They could hear the fanfare as he proudly entered the gates surrounding the council city, declaring that the war was over. Adoration and praise rained down on him as he rode through the streets on his way to what was left of the council hall.

"We are saved!" bellowed Bestos, with more tired relief than excitement.

"Where is it?" Replied Millen, his voice lacking as much relief as his Eastern counterpart.

"What? The snake? How should I know? Jori will tell us in a matter of minutes. The important thing is that we are saved!" His attempts to lighten what had become a dark and sour mood fell flat.

"We must decide what to do now. We can't have that thing around, it's just not safe, he could rule the combined lands with that by his side."

"I'm sure he'll do no such thing. We will decide what happens next, all of us. In the council hall, like we always have."

"And what if he disagrees? You've seen how he gets when we don't give him what he wants. And how can we say no now?"

"Yes, that is a concern. But let's hear his story and we can go from there. Why worry about what could be, one thing is for certain… We are safe. The war is over!"

Exclamations like this usually resulted in a cheer at the very least. Bestos' words were only met with worried eyes and raised eyebrows. To the Northern leaders, the threat had not been removed, but replaced. Each one of them had borne witness to the power of that mystical creature, the likes of which they had never seen before. They had never laid eyes on the barbarians after they emerged from that cave, so this serpent was the biggest threat to life they had ever seen, or could ever imagine.

15

A NEW AGE

Jori burst through the door with deserved confidence and swagger, however his demeanour was misplaced and his entrance misjudged. The remaining councillors had already seen him enter through the space in the building that the wall used to occupy. All notions of humility and modesty that Jori had planned during his return journey had vanished. He was right to feel good about his victory, as it was the largest and most significant that any of the four realms had seen. Despite their unease, the councillors summoned enough false congratulations to leave Jori feeling validated as he took his place at the council table; a table that had clearly seen renovations since Jori and the serpent exited the hall.

"Congratulations, you have saved us all!" the flatness in his voice made Millen sound sarcastic. Jori could not notice.

"Thank you, good sirs. I am tired and weary, but the task is done." Jori was playing the part of victorious general well.

"We shall get you some food, you should rest." Offered Bestos in a friendly tone.

"Thank you."

"…and what of the guards? And your horse?" Millen was avoiding the subject of the serpent, unknowingly hitting a nerve.

"Ah, yes… well… unfortunately, it wasn't all plain sailing. There were complications."

"Complications?" Bestos had retained his friendly manner so that he wouldn't upset a tired and powerful Jori.

"Yes, some of the beasts broke through and got to the men. They fought valiantly, but none survived. A terrible shame."

"But you did." The spike in Millen's voice had become noticeable   now.

"Well… yes… but I… I almost didn't. The serpent saved me just in time."

"Just you?" Millen was leaning forward now "…It did not save one single guard, but only yourself… why?"

"I was further back. When the monsters got close, the men advanced, and I stayed up high to command the serpent. By the time they got near me, the serpent had spotted them and came to assist." Jori had expected this conversation, but not so soon. He had a full day of travel in anticipation of this meeting, his story was as watertight as he could make it. The council seemed satisfied with his answers in what was beginning to feel more like an interrogation than a debrief, let alone the reception of a victorious hero.

"And where is it now?" Bestos pondered, taking over the questioning from Millen, who was beginning to show his mistrust.

"He is outside the city walls. I didn't want to alarm the people."

"A wise decision. And you are able to command him of these things, are you?" Bestos looked around again, attempting to reassure his nervous fellow councillors. While he shared their concerns, he more than any, knew the importance of keeping them from Jori.

"Well, yes. I wouldn't say command exactly, but yes. If I will it, he will stay out of sight."

"So, what happens now, fearless saviour?" Millen's spite was becoming troublesome for both Jori and Bestos.

"Now, we celebrate. The war is won! Jori, you need some food, some rest, and a good…" Bestos stopped himself short. The three things had always been a package for him in times of celebration, but it was a matter of days since Lowena had been sacrificed. "And a good rest… You must be exhausted." Relief filled the room, Bestos had avoided provoking their new threat. No-one was more relieved than Jori, who was just happy to have successfully survived his first interrogation. It's true, he was exhausted, both physically and emotionally, but for now at least it seemed as if he was in the clear.

In stark contrast to the chaotic few days before Jori set out east, the days that followed were long. The events had taken their toll on the councillors, none more so than Jori.

With the celebrations of his recent glory now a hazy memory, Jori's thoughts had turned to Lowena. Outside of the endless discussions of the council, Jori felt hollow. A piece of him had now gone, and it needed to be replaced. Rebuilding his empire could not be the same now that she had left him; Nothing would be. But it was here that Jori decided to place his efforts. With everything the last two years had taught him, he would be able to create an empire for himself that the world had never seen, a city in his image reminding future generations of the sacrifices he and his wife had made to allow them a future.

With his new purpose driving him once again, he set about negotiations. Now he had a purpose, the discussions were more efficient; he knew what he wanted and he knew how to get it. Jori's land was fertile and prosperous, but it was primitive. He demanded the latest technology from the northern scientists and machinery from the industrialists. With this, Jori could build the most advanced city in the four realms. From the witches, he demanded access to books and literature to understand their world better. The councillors agreed instantly to his requests, though they saw them more as demands. Their prompt agreement left Jori surprised; these were not easy men to negotiate with. "So that's it then? You all agree? Even you Millen?"

"Yes, we all agree. On one condition." Millen spoke in a rehearsed manner, giving Falmond his cue.

Falmond's absence had been notable ever since he left the great hall just before Jori and the serpent had. The northern leaders had attributed this to cowardice; unlike them, he was not a strong or brave man, and they had seen the way he was with the witches. This was partly true; what Falmond had seen that day had affected him deeply, along with the death of his fellow witches. He had not been, as the northerners had suggested 'cowering in his quarters', but instead theorising and pondering the next stage of mankind's ever-changing journey. He had conceived various outcomes for the situation, none of which involved Jori's failure. He had seen the serpent, but he had *felt* its power, success was a certainty in Falmond's eyes, which gave him a head start.

"One condition? Name it." Jori's suspicions grew. He knew what the condition would be and he didn't like it. Jori's powerful new creature had been roaming the lands outside the city for days now, and he could feel its impatience. He couldn't risk its presence damaging his position in negotiations; and in truth he had very little use for it now that their safety was ensured.

"The serpent Jori. We must do something about the serpent. We can't have a creature like that roaming wild. We don't know what it could do."

"What could it do? You tell me, you're the wizard. I'll tell you what it will do, whatever I command, That's what." Jori had begun to lose his temper.

"Yes, and just what would that be?" snarked Millen, who judging by the faces of the other men, had been instructed to stay quiet.

"To protect us. To keep us safe, in case something like this happens again. Don't you forget, if it wasn't for that serpent, and my Jul…."

"Alright, alright. We understand Jori." Bestos soothed, desperately trying to keep things on track.

"I'm not killing it." Jori's composure was hanging by a thread. Falmond continued.

"No one is asking you to kill it Jori, just to…" From the looks directed at the old wizard, it was clear; they *were* asking him to kill it. Falmond knew better. "We're just asking you to contain it. To keep somewhere safe."

"Safe?"

"Yes. We need to keep the creature safe from anyone who would want to take advantage of its power. We also need to keep people safe from…"

"But I control it. It will not kill or attack unless I command it."

"Are you sure Jori?" Falmond had not been present at Jori's homecoming interrogation, and questions of the men and his horse had never been brought to light since that day. If Falmond did know something, he didn't elaborate further, and Jori didn't want to push him.

"Yes, I am certain. Look… I understand your fears, I do. But this is something that we need to keep with us. There's nothing that will challenge the peace and security of the realms again while the serpent is still alive."

"Unless you command it." Millen could no longer control his bile. "What's stopping you from wanting the four realms for yourself. Like you said… nothing will challenge it!"

"You'll have to trust me. Isn't that why we're here? I trust all of you and I would hope you trust me. If that is not the case then we have a bigger problem on our hands." Jori's assuredness made the men uneasy, if things were not peacefully resolved here and now, there could be drastic consequences. There would be no war, but there would certainly be death. The northern men knew this, and so did Jori.

"We trust you Jori." Falmond intervened. Aware of the thin ice that they stood on, the northern men sat back and left the wizard to calm Jori's rising temper.

"Then what do you propose? What is your *condition*?"

"That the serpent is kept somewhere. Somewhere safe and peaceful, away from the people."

"You mean hidden? Like a secret?"

"A secret, Jori? Not like a secret, no. But to have your people living in the fear of that thing would only end in disaster. It was created for one purpose, and for that purpose it needed power. Now that power is too much for peaceful times. You must choose between peace, and the serpent." "Well, I choose peace. Of course, I choose peace." Jori didn't hesitate. Falmond's slow delivery had allowed Jori time to ponder his words. His kind yet knowing eyes filled Jori with uncertainty, bringing thoughts of his muddy epiphany back to him. "I mean no harm. I am burdened with this; it is my responsibility. I won't kill it, and I won't mistreat it. I will take it far out and keep it away from people."

"That is both a wise and considerate decision Jori, thank you."

This was clearly one of the outcomes that Falmond had considered acceptable during his isolated musings during the last few days. The second was an idea that shaped the world as we know it today. He addressed the crowd with a newfound confidence, not that of an elderly wizard; almost mimicking the great Bestos. His chest had puffed out under his beard and his stance was much wider, a technique that he had borrowed from Jori when he had tried to look taller.

"The events of the last few days have been nothing short of extraordinary. Even for a seasoned mystic such as myself, these last days have been almost inexplicable. But we find ourselves on the precipice of a new world. A world that only exists today because of the actions and decisions of this council. Every one of you has had a hand in securing our survival, and every one of you should have a hand in shaping our future. The realms of the world are many, and they are scattered. I propose that we join these lands and meet as we have been."

"Join them how?" Asked Bestos, who was unsure, but not averse to the notion.

"It's clear, to me at least, that we have five distinct cultural groupings. The South East, we know an unfortunate amount about. It will require a great deal of rebuilding, and much of the magic has been destroyed. The North East leads us all in science and innovation. The North West is unmatched when it comes to industry and manufacturing. The South West is fertile and rich in agriculture. In addition to these four areas, the city surrounding the council hall has blossomed into a thriving financial hub, and one of the finest cities in the lands. If I have learned anything over the last two years, it's that we can achieve a lot more by working together. We all have something that we need from each other, and we hold something that the others need. This can only lead to equal and fair trading across the lands."

"That's an interesting proposal Falmond." Millen had taken a more intellectual pose that he usually did, or so he thought. "…Who would lead these new kingdoms? There can be no kingdom without a king, and I count nine kings and five kingdoms.

"Ah, yes, well that is the predicament. As I see it, and by no means it this doctrine, a mere suggestion if you will… I would take charge of the rebuilding in the South East, Jori would reign in the South West, and for his commendable work in setting up this fine city around us, Liston would rule over the Middle kingdom where we are now."

"And the North?" Bestos' accent had become much more pronounced in his delivery, only serving to emphasise the divide.

"Well, that's the issue. I would suggest that you would rule the North-East and Millen the North-West, but that does leave us with four northern councillors with no kingdoms. We could divide the north further, creating six smaller northern kingdoms? The North is far bigger than the South."

"Smaller and weaker" spiked Millen "You'd like that! Divide us up and watch us suffer. No… we will rule, and we will make lords of our fellow councillors. We shall rule with their assistance. Unlike you southerners, we have no ego that stands in our path." He lied, but did so convincingly. The other northern councillors agreed. The last few years had seen a noticeable power shift to the newly appointed Kings, challenging this now would be as foolish as attacking the South-West and Jori's serpent.

So, it was decided. Five kingdoms, five kings, four Lords. One serpent, three heads.

Jori was both flattered and excited. A kingdom. His own kingdom. He stood outside the council hall and waved the new leaders farewell as they left, each of them seemingly less overwhelmed with their new positions than he was. The longer he stood there, the more the gravity of his new title weighed down on him. A king? He thought. A king of what? What is left? Before his thoughts could spiral into panic, a soft voice cut them short.

"Jori?"

"Ah, Falmond… Quite the task we have ahead of us isn't it?"

"Indeed. None more so than yourself."

"I don't know, I can't see the northern alliance being an easy ordeal to manage." Falmond smiled knowingly.

"No, but I'm sure they will shout their way to a suitable outcome."

"Good luck to them."

"They aren't the only ones I worry about though."

"No, me neither. Liston is a capable man, but I am concerned about his leadership qualities, although I suppose that the kingdom is nearly half built by now anyway."

"You Jori. I'm concerned for you."

"Me? I have fertile land and strong people, we will build a fine kingdom… don't you worry about me."

"You know what I am referring to." The smug grin slowly melted from Jori's face.

"Leave that to me. I shall obey the council's orders and keep it locked away. Have no fear, old man. The last thing I need in my kingdom is that thing running riot."

"And if it decides otherwise?"

"It will not. It shares my will. If I want it to stay away, it will."

"Well, that may be so… But just in case…"

"Do you not trust me? After all we have been through? The sacrifices I have made?" Jori's tone had turned, and Falmond knew better than to fan the flames of Jori's anger.

"I have a gift." He said in the friendliest possible way. "Two gifts actually."

"Oh. I'm sorry. I didn't mean to react like that. Thank you Falmond."

"I'm not saying that anything untoward would happen, but just in case it does."

"What are they?"

"Weapons. Well, one is. A sword and an amulet. The most powerful weapons we possess."

"Then why are you giving them to me? Surely you will need them?"

"We have defeated our foes Jori. There is only one threat left to the five kingdoms." He softened his eyes apologetically at Jori, who was visibly annoyed again, but he managed to suppress it this time.

"Thank you. Like I said, you need not worry, but I can't stop you. If this makes you feel better, then I will take good care of them. Thank you."

Falmond handed over a package, wrapped up in dark brown cloth and tied together with black ribbon, the two men shared an awkward handshake. Falmond made his uneasy retreat away from the council and Jori looked down at his package. He could feel the power of what lay wrapped within; he hoped that he would never need to use it.

16

BACK TO THE FUTURE

In the decades that followed his world changing years with the council, Jori set about his new mission with all the vigour and determination that you would expect of a man desperately seeking to fill an empty void. Without Lowena, Jori had to keep himself in check; a task that he had never truly managed.

Work kept him busy enough for his mind to keep from straying too far. In many ways, Jorisham was a shrine to his lost love, the natural gardens an ode to her love of the living world, the way all workers were treated a reflection of the values and beliefs that drove her. The city was filled with altruism and benevolence. No wealth could be gained at the expense of others and those who were struggling would receive assistance in their plight. It was a primitive form of social welfare, but it worked. At the heart of it all, the part of the city dedicated to all those things that Lowena loved; Lowston. The place where like-minded individuals could explore creativity and ponder the larger questions of eternal existence that occupied Lowena so much and entirely passed Jori by.

On the days that his emotions got the better of him, Jori had several places he could go to clear his mind. The first of these was the darkest. At the furthest point west, where giant cliffs overlooked the inhospitable ocean, Jori would visit his most feared secret. He had declared the lands surrounding the bay sacred, and for as long as anyone could remember, no one had dared go near. Despite thriving and spreading throughout the other Kingdoms, religion had never been promoted in Jorisham. Lowston was the ideal place for all matters to be discussed, but no time was given to allowing these ideas to become doctrine in wider Jorisham. Jori's journeys west were viewed by those around him as some kind of ancient ritual, one that they were grateful to be spared.

Since the mystical events of the final battle, Jori had lived a life longer than any mortal he knew. His unexplained longevity meant that several generations had come and gone while Jori had moved from middle into old age. During this time, the stories and details of the battle had turned to legend, and legend had turned to myth. Generations after the five kingdoms had been formed, the knowledge of these events had only been passed down by those who could remember. Jori's wild tales of giant serpents and barbarian monsters were rightfully dismissed as hyperbole or metaphor. His actions and their consequence though, remained trusted and respected.

On those cliffs, Jori would usually catch a glimpse of the serpent, who could sense his presence from afar. Far below, he could see it battling waves, catching fish, or sleeping in the caves under the cliffs. Jori shared the discomfort felt by the snake. It was not imprisoned here, but they both knew that the serpent wasn't free. As Jori slowly began to grow into old age, his thoughts during these visits would turn to his imminent demise. What would happen to the serpent when he was gone? Would it roam free and destroy everything that he had created? Would it die as well? He may be linked to the creature, but its life source came not from Jori, but Lowena. While these thoughts troubled Jori, these frequent visits served as a poignant reminder. They reminded him of what could have been, of what he could become. He always headed back east to the kingdom with a renewed resolve and determination, refocussed on his goal to create the greatest kingdom in the lands, a memorial to his wife, a testament to his own success.

While the coastal trips hid a dark secret, his late-night visits to Lowston satisfied his more ignoble urges. Jori did not take another wife in this new era of progress. If he had, his long life would subject him to once again watching them pass on before him, no matter their age. This was not something that Jori could bear to suffer again, so he stayed alone in his grand castle, warm memories of Lowena flickering in the dark.

The last of his solaces was his most obvious. Thanks to the technological advancements brought from the North-East combined with the agricultural prowess of his Jorisham farmers, Jori had secured a plentiful supply of the realm's finest ale. The kingdom brewery grew to a powerhouse of industry and kept many of the city's people employed. Inside the royal castle, the highest generals, the most noble gentry, and the wealthiest businessmen would gather night after night in the Grand Hall.

The hall was a different place when Jori was present, regaling his guests with fanciful stories of the times before the kingdoms. Entertaining them all with whimsical tales of wizards and witches, giant fire eagles and his glorious battles. Jori would ensure that he never told the same story twice, this way he kept his tales in the realms of fiction and allowed himself endless evenings of adoration from his guests. The further the evenings progressed, the further Jori would stray from reality, his absurd repartee served as the comic centrepiece of the great halls unparalleled ambience.

17

ALL GOOD THINGS

Jori's days of building and planning, of drinking and of storytelling had come to an end. Despite how he felt, even in old age, Jori was never alone. Through his years he had amassed a considerable number of loyal serving staff, devoted and faithful. They went about their duties in the open, sharing long and intimate conversations with the king. With no wife, these staff members had become his family. Jori was no fool, he knew the friendship he shared with the guests at the great hall was fleeting, he had seen so many of them come and go over the years. More an audience than companions, they served a purpose but did little to fill the chasm of companionship left by his wife's sacrifice.

At the heart of the castle, Mrs. Buxhall and Mrs. Haughley ran the service staff. Two large, kind ladies who had taken a role in the castle from their mothers. Mrs. Buxhall and Mrs. Haughley grew up in the castle, under the stewardship of the king. He had always treated them with kindness and compassion and they rewarded him with their loyal service. The two ladies knew little of life outside the castle, and neither did they want to. Their lives provided them with everything they needed; food, security, company, and entertainment. The kitchens and service rooms were always a buzz of excitement and light-hearted camaraderie. The staff themselves were a close-knit family, not one of them able to gain employment without the authorisation of these matriarchs, all except Mrs. Felsam, who had recently joined during a staff shortage, but had a glowing recommendation from her predecessor.

The closest two staff members to the king were brother and sister, Calia and Viga, the quarter staff. While Viga was the closest to Jori, dressing him, and carrying out his personal errands, it was Calia who Jori confided in most. Calia was young, but not naïve. She had grown up in the harder parts of Lowston and was orphaned at an early age. Together with her older brother Viga, they had gained employment in the castle through their Aunt, who had become close with Mrs. Haughley. Calia had worked for the king since she was a small girl and although the vast, empty castle of a lonely king was not an ideal place for a young girl, she had a safe and happy childhood there. From that early age, she had earned her place in the castle staff through her hard work and compassion. Viga by contrast was neither competent nor reliable, traits Jori accommodated begrudgingly, much to the exasperation of the other staff.

Jori's noticeable fondness for Calia raised a few eyebrows among some of the newer recruits to the castle staff, but were shut down immediately by their superiors; they knew better. Jori's fondness for Calia was felt and shared by all other long serving staff members. To insinuate that his affection for any of them was anything more than plutonic was tantamount to treason, and after any amount of time spent in the castle with Jori, any doubters would soon dispel any of these misconceptions.

For Jori, he always tried to run his house in the way that Lowena would have. In their life together, the two of them had never dreamed of having serving staff, and Jori would often muse over what Lowena would make of his lavish new life. The luxuries that Jori's life as a monarch granted him were beyond anything that he would have been able to imagine as a simple farmer, and in truth he never got used to this lifestyle. In relation to other kings, Jori's life was unremarkable and humble. Aside from the budget allocated to ale, his spending was thrifty and his luxuries were modest. Jori did not want for anything, but his demands were always modest, especially for a king.

As the years marched on, Jori grew weary. After all these years, it seemed that time had caught up with him at last. Gradually, his frequent appearances in the castle hall became rarer, until one day they ceased altogether. The only people who knew the reason behind Jori's absence were of course. his closest companions… his staff.

"What's going on sir, you haven't touched your stew. Mrs. Buxhall will take it out on me if I don't take it back empty." Calia's large, dark eyes could not hide her increasing sadness as seeing Jori's frame wither before her. For a man who had barely aged in decades, seeing age devour him so quickly was something that she could not prepare herself for.

"Just take it down, it's OK. Just tell her that I'm not hungry, and apologise."

"She won't have it, you know she won't. She'll think you don't like it and make you something else. So, you might as well just eat this." They shared a warm smile, the solemnity of the situation resonating between them.

"You know her too well. And me. There's no hiding from you. I'll have a bit, and do my best, as long as you agree to tip what I don't eat down the drain".

Calia gave one of her defiant looks, but as she stared hard into the old man's eyes, she could see how fragile he had become. This was not the time for one of their stubborn but light-hearted disagreements, this was the time for compassion; a trait Calia held in excess. With neither king nor maid acknowledging the situation they were in, it weighed heavily on them. As Calia brought the spoon up to Jori's weakened mouth, they continued to avoid each other's eyes, as if by doing they would deny the bleak reality of their circumstance.

The next morning, it was Mrs. Buxhall who Jori awoke to, not Calia. Sharply sweeping open the curtains, she turned and addressed Jori with more than a hint of sternness. "Good morning sir, I hope that you have rested well?"

"Well, not w..."

"Good..." Mrs. Buxhall interjected "...Because there is no time for moping about and sleeping. You are a king, and there is work to be done." Mrs. Buxhall was speaking far beyond her station. Both king and cook knew that this was not the correct way to address such a powerful monarch. Both also knew that this is how Mrs. Buxhall had always addressed him, and that he had always allowed it. Jori was quick to anger and those who approached him did so with caution, from general to farmer; but not Mrs. Buxhall... she knew him better than that. "I know what's going on, and I know you're not well." Jori cast an eye to Calia, standing awkwardly in the corner accompanied by Mrs. Felsam. "It wasn't her. Do you think us fools Your Majesty? I have known you and this castle my entire life. Any change in you… I see it. Anything out of place here… *I see it.* And you slope around hardly able to stand and expect me not to notice?"

"I didn't want to alarm or upset anyone." Jori had known Mrs. Buxhall since she was a baby. For her to grow into late middle age had put them on an equal standing where age was concerned, but he was now much older and much frailer than her.

"Well, we are upset. Of course, we are. You've clearly not got much longer left, and you're not going to leave us like this sir." Mrs. Buxhall was a caring woman, a deeply loving and gentle soul, but had never been good at expressing this. A younger Jori would have revelled in calling out her lack of tact, which he had fortunately always found endearing. Now, her words fell hard on him, their truth weighing down on his feeble frame.

"Leave us like what?" The defiance and stubbornness that Jori usually showed when confronted in this manner had been replaced by a calm acceptance.

"Without a leader. If you go, then who will lead? One of your oafish friends in the hall? One of the servants?"

"What do you suggest?" Mrs. Buxhall was taken back; she had not prepared for this. She had prepared herself to confront him and force him to present them with his solution. She expected him to have a plan, lying bed all day, she had assumed that's what he had been thinking about. In reality, Jori's head was a swirling mess of the past; of victories and defeats, triumphs and mistakes… and of the serpent. Had he been selfish not to think of the kingdom's future, just because it would no longer contain himself.

She was right, he thought… as she often was. Her insight was limited, but when she had an opinion, it was often a good one. What kind of king would he be remembered as, if he deserted his people at the last moment, leaving them open to attack or misdirection? His people were simple, loyal, and easy to lead.

"If only you had an heir to your throne Your Majesty, all of this would be a lot easier to resolve. You could appoint them your successor and that would be that." Her comforting tone was bordering on patronising.

"Well, I don't. Do I? Don't give me hypothetical nonsense Mrs. Buxhall. Give me solutions." Jori's tone was short, abrupt, and unexpected.

"Very well sir, I didn't mean to offend. I shall leave you in peace." Mrs. Buxhall took her leave, glaring back intensely at the tray of food she had prepared.

"She means well, Your Majesty. You know she's not good at expressing herself properly." Calia soothed him and brought up his tray of food ready to feed him once more.

"I know she's right, but I just don't know what the solution is."

18

AN UNUSUAL SOLUTION

It had been days since Mrs. Buxhall had challenged her king. Neither herself nor Jori could formulate a solution, which prevented them from raising the issue again. The castle carried on, in hushed tones and quiet contemplation.

Winter had begun to take hold of the large castle, which felt colder this year than any before it. Jori's time in his quarters had turned from feeble moping to frantic and desperate searching. He could feel that time was running out for him to find a solution. Driven almost to despair by his isolated brooding, he had to ease his muddled mind. For the first time since he had discovered it, Jori had not touched a drop of ale in weeks, the thought alone made him sick to his stomach. His other solace required far too much activity and would likely hasten his departure at this late stage. He had to visit it, just one last time.

Mrs. Felsam Was preparing a fire in his sleeping quarters, waiting for him to arise so that she could summon

Viga to assist him. "Mrs. Err...F"
"Felsam Your Majesty" She said with a cowering half-curtsy.
The king had never directly addressed her before, as she was
new, but prior to his sudden decline they had both engaged
in group conversations together.

"Yes, sorry, Mrs. Felsam, can you please prepare a
carriage? I would like to go on a trip."

"Of course, Your Majesty."

"And... and please don't tell Calia or the others."
"Of course sir, but they will be concerned for your safety.
What should I tell them?"

"Just tell them I've gone for fresh air."

"How long will you be?"

"Just a day or so I imagine. Carriages aren't as fast as a
lone horse."

"A day? I don't think Mrs. Buxhall will allow it."
"Allow it? I'm the king. I fear she forgets that sometimes."
"Of course Your Majesty. She will just worry, that is all."
"Well, I won't be alone, you will come with me. Would that
suit the 'lady of the house'?"

"I imagine she will have stern words with me when we
return, but if that's what you command, then what can she
do?"
"Exactly."
"May I ask, your highness... where we will be going?"

"West. Just tell the driver 'West'."

They set off at once. The carriage was blisteringly cold.
Jori was wrapped in as many blankets as Mrs. Felsam had
managed to sneak out of the castle without rousing suspicion.
The cold air hung awkwardly between them, Mrs. Felsam's
mind an obvious whirlwind of questions.

"How long have you been with us?"

"Just over a year."

"Well, I don't feel like I know you well at all. Did you grow up in Jorisham?"

"No, I moved here when I was Twenty."

"Oh, that's exciting, but more common these days I suppose. Where did you move from?"

Mrs. Felsam would much rather be asking the questions, but she knew her place and was grateful for the lack of silence.

"From the East, a town called Laakso, just west of Kituo."

"Ah, Kituo. I will never forget my time in Kituo with the council, Well… Before it was called that."

"None of us will forget your time there, Your Majesty." Mrs. Felsam's earnest remark had been misconstrued as sarcasm, which did not please Jori.

"Well, if it wasn't for my time there with the council, and my acts in battle, you wouldn't be here now. None of us would."

"I know your highness, that was what I meant. Forgive me, I misspoke. I was merely saying that your time there should never be forgotten."

"Oh, right, well yes… I agree with you on that."

"So, the witch's realm 'eh?... I am a keen student of their ways. Are you a witch Mrs. Felsam?" Jori joked, attempting to cover his previous misjudged reaction.

"No Sir. In truth, witches are hard to find in the East these days."

"Too right, off travelling the world, using their powers for their own gain so I hear." Mrs. Felsam was silent. Jori had misspoken again. The brash assumptions that are thrown around ale-soaked dining halls may not be the most diplomatic opinions for a king to hold, or to speak of.

"Anyway, they are a good sort. I was friends with a witch once. Wonderful woman."

"Oh yes, I think I have heard of your time with the witches in the council, Heilmur? Wasn't that her name?"

"Very good! Yes. That was her. Vahvuus and Henki as well, although I'll admit that we were less close. And of course, the almighty Falmond 'The Healer'. I shared a lot of time with him as well."

"That's very impressive your highness. I have heard of them all through the stories, powerful and brave, all of them."
"So what brought you here?"

"The west can be a hard place to live, especially if you possess no powers. It's a cold and loveless place in truth."

"So, a man? That's why you ventured West? For love?" Jori's questioning had made her uneasy. Is this what he had brought her away from the castle for? To give him an Heir? Jori noticed her face turn cold. King or not, his line of questioning was not appropriate for a man of his age, especially to someone in his employment. "Sorry, I didn't mean to pry. I just find travel fascinating. Since my days in the council, I have never stepped foot outside my own kingdom."

"It's ok." She said, a wave of relief swept over her, the awkward air thickened in the carriage once more.

By the time they got to the cliffs, Mrs. Felsam had fallen asleep. Barely able to hold himself, Jori clambered down from the carriage with the help of the guard. He made his way over to cliff, instructing the guard in no uncertain terms to stay where he was.

The wind struck him hard as he approached the edge of the precipice. He sat down for fear of getting swept away and shuffled closer to the edge. Down below, he caught sight of the serpent, as strong as ever, flying up and diving back down into the crashing waves. He watched as it rose and fell with a rhythm he knew all too well. Its presence gave him great comfort, their shared past kept hidden from the world all this time. The creature had always puzzled him and occupied so many of his thoughts. Looking down, marvelling once again at the raw power of the snake, he could not escape an uneasy feeling. If he was so frail, how was the serpent still so powerful?

"It's real." If Jori were standing, he would have fallen to certain death. Mrs. Felsam was standing behind him wrapped in a blanket, her eyes filled with awe and wonder.

"Mrs. Felsam, what are you doing here? I said you must stay in the carriage. This… this is simply not acceptable." Jori was obviously flustered. For decade after decade, this had been a refuge that Jori had kept from even his closest companions. Now, in his final days, his secret was out.

As they were carried home in silence, Jori began to feel a sense of relief wash over him. After all these years, he could finally talk to someone about this. Yes, he had spun yarns of the serpent and its terrifying power, but he had told many more about other fantastic creatures that had never existed. Every fanciful notion that he had concocted with the witches was magically brought to life through his natural gift for fabrication and embellishment. Now, he could talk with openness and honesty.

"You don't seem as shocked as I thought you would be." He said.

"I suppose not. I don't know what I was expecting, really. It was quite far away, but still… what an incredible creature." "I almost lost my head when I first saw it, I don't mind admitting."

"I can imagine. But those were different times, and like I said, I grew up around witches."

"Do they have things like that in the South-East then?"

"No." She laughed "Not at all. But I had heard the stories and always imagined it. In the East I've seen things you would struggle to believe."

"I suppose you're just not easy to shock then?"

"I suppose not." She paused "Are you?"

"Well, not anymore. I'm too tired to be shocked these days… what's the point?"

"I wouldn't bet on it Your Majesty."

"Ha, now there's a challenge to brighten up our journey home. Give me your best shot." Jori had perked up considerably and was almost glowing with excitement. The last few weeks had been agonisingly dreary and serious. A bit of fun is just what he needed. Mrs. Felsam did not glow. Her mood darkened and her face cast a serious frown.

"I'm not sure that's a good idea."

"Oh, come on… it's too early to chicken out. I thought you had something shocking up your sleeve? Or were you calling my bluff Mrs. Felsam? As your king, I command you. Shock me. Shock me to my very core." Jori had not been this jubilant in several weeks.

"Very well. What if I was to tell you…?" She paused again.

"Yes, what is it? Buying yourself some time?" Jori had leaned in closer, his childish look beginning to irritate Mrs. Felsam.

"What if I told you that there was a way of you claiming an Heir? An heir with you as a father and it's mother…"

"…It's mother?" The childish look had evaporated from Jori's face, but he was still eagerly leaning towards her.

"Lowena. If Lowena were its mother and you were its father."

"Well, I wouldn't be shocked at all." Said Jori sitting back in his seat, the excitement fading from his frail bones. "I wouldn't be shocked, because that's not possible. Mrs. Felsam, you have used my emotions unfairly. I wanted to be shocked, not unnecessarily upset."

"But your highness; there is a way."

Jori leaned in again. He could tell by her grave expression that she was not intentionally upsetting him, and that she was serious.

"That creature, born out of sacrifice and love. Love between you and Lowena."

"That serpent is not my child Mrs. Felsam. Not by any stretch of the imagination. We have a connection, a bond if you will, but not like that."

"Yes, but it *could* be. It could be your child your highness."

"You are starting to talk in riddles Mrs. Felsam, and bordering on the absurd. You had better start making sense soon, or I am going to get very upset indeed."

"I know it sounds unusual, and it is. But from what I have heard of the stories of how the creature came into being… it's possible to…"

"From what you've heard? From who? Those aren't the stories I tell; I never mention my Lowena in the stories *I* tell. What stories are you speaking of?" Jori had become noticeably defensive.

"In the East. Just fairy tales and myths."

"Myths indeed. I don't know what you think you know about my serpent, but I suggest that we end this conversation here."

They rode on, the tension between them hard and cold as ice. The journey back from the coast felt considerably longer than their journey out, the pressure of words unsaid filling them both to the point of bursting. It was just outside the kingdom that Jori surrendered to his curiosity.

"So, you're telling me that there is a way of turning my serpent into my heir, so that he may reign over the Kingdom in my absence?"

"Yes."

"An actual human person, whom I can talk to and guide? To shape in my own image?"

"I Suppose so. I don't know the 'ins and outs' of it all, but I know that it's possible."

"How? How do you know? I have many books on the subject of witchcraft, given to me my no less than Falmond 'The Healer'. There is no talk of such a spell in those books."

"That is old magic, this is… well, it is a more contemporary art form."

"Contemporary. That doesn't fill me with confidence. I may not be so distrusting of new ways as I used to be, but I still don't like the sound of it."

"What have you got to lose?" Those words felt like a sharp slap on Jori's cold face. He knew that his time was running out, so did the whole castle; until now it had always seemed like a gentle inevitability. The reminder that he had nothing to pass on, nothing to protect, was not pleasant. All the things that Jori held dear lived and died with him. He fell silent for some time.

"Make whatever plans you need to and I will have my answer for you tomorrow." He said as they entered the castle gates.

"As you wish, Your Majesty."

19

RETURNING EAST

The decision to explore Mrs. Felsam's idea had been an easy one for Jori to make. The lack of other options had opened his mind to the concept, but with each passing hour in the last day his curiosity had grown exponentially. By the time they set off east the following afternoon, Jori was giddy with excitement. Far from the sceptical and defensive travelling companion she had shared her previous trip to the coast with, Jori was a twitching ball of nervous anticipation. To say that he had been given a new lease of life was an understatement, he had finally begun to look like his old self.

The convoy that accompanied them was anything but inconspicuous. Jori had given the staff at the castle an elaborate story of going to retrieve some new machinery from the North-East. A story that was not believed fully by a single member of staff. Jori had long since delegated this type of duty to those beneath him, and had not set foot out of Jorisham in decades. Nonetheless, he was their king, and as such, his word was the undisputable truth. Despite Mrs. Felsam's insistence, she and Jori were not accompanied by any guards, their only companions their two drivers; one for their large carriage and one for the enormous industrial carriage behind them, the longest and tallest in the kingdom.

It was early evening by the time they reached the cove where the serpent had resided for so many years. Mrs. Felsam was instructed to stay inside her carriage, which she both heard and obeyed this time. Trips to the western coast had always filled Jori with a sense of peace and familiarity. Now, standing at the edge of the world looking down as he had so many times before, he became increasingly aware that this would be his last visit west. This sacred place that held so much significance for him would be nothing without the serpent, and with his days as finite as they were, he doubted whether he would have the time or inclination to return. This feeling only intensified Jori's drive to see out his final chapter to completion and ensure the safety of the realm. With the power possessed by the serpent ruling over his kingdom, the people would be safe and his legacy would be eternal.

It had been generations since Jori had commanded the snake. During visits, he would watch it crashing into waves, he would feel its movements and gently manipulate them… but he had never given a specific command. He began to question whether he had ever given a full command to the serpent, or whether it had just shared the same goals as him. He consoled himself with the fact that the creature had stayed in that cove for decade after decade, never venturing out. That was a command, a command that he had given. *Of course, I can still command him*, he thought, dispelling his reservations and steadying his hands.

105

With one sharp move, Jori gestured towards the back of the long open carriage. Within seconds, the serpent was inside. Jori had forgotten how quickly it could move and how agile it was. He had also forgotten just how big it was. From high upon the cliff looking down, the serpent's power and size was a true spectacle, but up close it was unimaginable. The drivers closed the door on the serpent, trembling with fear and confusion, but carrying out their orders with steely determination. They had been paid well for this unusual expedition, and they were beginning to see why. The doors were shut and the serpent was only just contained; bulging the sides and almost buckling the many wheels of the enormous carriage.

The journey east was long and dark. Each day, they would take shelter and conceal the carriage, only traveling under the cover of darkness. In these new modern times, one sighting of the serpent would spread throughout the kingdom like wildfire, leaving Jori with a lot of explaining to do. By the time they reached the witch's realm, it had been eight days. For any other man of Jori's age and condition, the expedition would have surely been their end, but not Jori. Jori had work to do, his one final push before he would allow death to take him. That famous drive that brought the success that he had seen his whole life, the same drive that last brought him east; one last stand.

It was an hour before dawn when they finally reached their destination. At the entrance to the cave, stood three ghostly, thin women.

"We're here Jori" Mrs. Felsam whispered. Jori had slept through most days, and what he could of the nights. It wasn't easy to sleep in a moving carriage, his brittle bones rattling against the hard wood of the carriage.

"Thank goodness for that." He said, his weary face catching the cold gaze of the three women. "Is that them? The witches who can do this?"

"Yes, that's them. Necerta, Frigus and Stulta."

"Well I'll do my best to remember that, but I do struggle with witches' names."

"It has been some time Your Majesty."

"You're not wrong there. Although I don't even think I've travelled this far east. Is this Laakso, your hometown?"

"No, your highness, we are much further east than that."

"Oh, well I've certainly never been this far then. Where are…"

"Good morning Your Majesty." The tallest witch cut him off, growing impatient with their conversation.

"Oh, yes, sorry. Good morning. I am King Jori of Jorisham."

"We Know." Said the tall, slender witch. Her face was thin and long like a fox. Her eyes were narrow but shapely. "We have been expecting you. I am Necerta, this is Frigus, and Stulta. We are here to grant your request Your Majesty." Frigus and Stulta coldly nodded their heads in acknowledgment of the king. Jori could hardly expect a warm welcome in the land of witches. Warmth was a trait seldom held by witches, especially with regard to strangers.

"Where is it?" Stulta asked. Stulta was as close as a witch could be to being considered 'beautiful'. She has softer features than a witch would usually have. Her rounded cheek bones and flatter nose a stark contrast to the jagged lines shared by the rest of her kind. Her skin was warmer and darker compared to the bright grey skin of her counterparts.

"Oh… straight to it. It's in the back there. I suppose you want to see it?"

"Obviously." Snarked Frigus, who even by witch's standards was cold. Her icy blue eyes showing not even the faintest attempt of friendliness.

"Shouldn't we discuss terms first?"

"Terms?" Necerta seemed surprised at his suggestion. "Well yes, how does this all work? What's going to happen?"

"You have come to us with a request, and we will grant you that request. For one thing in return."

"Yes, that's what I meant. That's the negotiation I was talking about." Jori was exasperated, after such a long journey and with no breakfast, he was not at all prepared for the harshness of witches. "What is your request?"

"Make no Mistake." Necerta said staring forcefully at him. "This is not a negotiation. You will get your heirs, and we will get what we want."

"And what do you want? Heirs? Surely you mean heir? I came to get one heir for my Kingdom, not multiple heirs."
"This creature is not one being. Not anymore. To transform it into human form will give three beings, one for each of the heads."

"Three heads? How do you know of the creature? I haven't showed it to you yet."

"We are witches Your Majesty. Witches know things." Necerta's delivery was sharp and unforgiving, but Jori kept his gaze fixed to her, avoiding the frozen glare of Frigus.

"Yes. Ok, I suppose you are right. And there is no way of only having one human from it?"

"Not without killing the other two. Is that something that you would like to do?" Necerta smirked, a welcome expression to Jori, desperate for some humanity to lighten the tone of the conversation.

"No, you are right there. I suppose that's fine, if it is the only way."

"It is."

"And what are these demands you speak of? What if I don't agree?"

"Don't agree? If you don't agree, then you have wasted your journey Your Majesty. You will just have to return home with that creature, and hope that no one catches sight of it on your way." Necerta's eyes showed him warmth for the first time, as if attempting to conceal the threat that was plainly laying beneath.

"So, what is it? What do you want?"

"There are three of us Your Majesty. Three witches… three heirs."

"Yes…"

"We would take each of your heirs as a husband and return west with you."

"Come and live as queens in Jorisham? No. You can't believe that I would agree to that?"

"Yes, of course. Do you wish your sons to die without an heir of their own? What will happen to Jorisham then?"

"Well, yes. I see your point. But they should choose their own wives. And we can't have queens that are…"

"Witches? Your Majesty?"

"I didn't mean it like that, but yes. There are no witches or wizards in Jorisham. We have balance and peace."

"You talk of balance. You know nothing of balance." Sneered Frigus. Despite Jori's best efforts, she had become involved once more. Jori puffed out his chest.

"I know more than you would believe young lady. How do you think this creature came to be? Don't tell me I don't know the sacrifices you witches need to power your magic.

109

So, tell me, who are we sacrificing this time? Are you going to take my life?"

"We both know that's not possible Your Majesty. Who would believe that they are your heirs if you were not there to tell them?" Jori began to relax. Having seen the level of sacrifice needed to create the serpent, he was happy not to relive the ordeal.

"Then what?"

"Magic has advanced since the days of Vahvuus, Heilmur and Henki. Our sacrifice would come from ourselves. We would sacrifice our powers." Jori had no time to dwell on their knowledge of the three witches and their sacrifice. Perhaps they had become legends in their own realm? Had Falmond told fables of his time in the council? Jori had hoped not. The events in that chaotic week painted none of them in a good light. It had been an unspoken agreement to draw attention away from their shortcomings and focus instead on the glory of their victory.

"You would give up your powers? Well, that works quite well in all of our favour really doesn't it."

"Quite so. You agree then? May we begin?"

Jori cast a hopeful look to Mrs. Felsam, who had done well to stay out of this tense discussion. She raised her eyebrows and nodded... that was all the guidance Jori needed. The serpent slithered carefully out of the large carriage and straight into the safety and seclusion of the cave. The drivers almost collapsed with relief and retreated to their seats. The witches were surprisingly unfazed by the sight of the serpent, leaving Jori a little disappointed. *Witches know things* he thought to himself sarcastically.

As he was so many years ago, Jori was excluded from the events that preceded the serpent's existence. Jori's inevitable fear and doubt were tinged with a sense of sadness. The creature that he had confided in over many generations would be no more. He had laid eyes upon its unfathomable form for the last time, and it hadn't looked back at him once. Now, he would only know what would emerge from within the cave. His head filled with fantasies about what his new sons could be. He pondered the new form of witchcraft that the witches had mastered and what this meant for the future. If no sacrifice of life was required for such a spell, then how would the balance he had learned of be kept? However fearful Jori felt of witchcraft, he at least believed that he understood it... All things must be equal.

He went over the equations in his head, trying to balance the formula. One serpent plus three withes equals three men and three witches. No. Three heads plus three witches equal three men and three witches. But where does the power come from? For Lowena, the process was simple; her life gave the creature life. The witches' lives and powers gave the serpent his three powerful heads. Four beings had merged to form one, with lives surrendered as currency to complete the process. Whatever was currently happening within that cave made no sense to Jori.

Whichever way he looked at it; they were short of one life. His mind turned grimly to Mrs. Felsam. Jori could not accept the idea that the witches could use their power instead of their lives, otherwise Lowena's life could have been spared. Witchcraft is as ancient as time and although many years had passed since Lowena's sacrifice, this was a mere second in relation to the timeline of witchcraft.

Time moved painfully slowly for Jori. He had spent the best part of a day ruminating over the puzzle that the witches had presented him with. His new travelling companion and dare he say it… friend, was inexplicably missing. She had accompanied them into the cave, and he had not questioned it. She was the one who had set this up, she was their common ally. When she had walked in with them, he had presumed she was going to speak with them or check that things were to her liking. He had never thought to question it. Now, several hours later and with no sign of Mrs. Felsam, that's all he could do.

By the time the witches emerged, Jori was beside himself with guilt and grief. He had allowed another person in his care to be sacrificed for his own means. When the four women returned, Jori collapsed, sobbing uncontrollably. The witches waited impatiently for him to regain composure, and finish his unnecessary outpouring of emotions. Jori collected himself and, arms stretched, approached Mrs. Felsam.

"Mrs. Felsam, my dear. I'm so glad to see you!" "Stop." Said Frigus sharply. "Mrs. Felsam is tired. And you have more important matters to attend. We don't have all day and I'm not going to waste any more of my time watching your endless histrionics." Jori was shocked. He did not consider his reaction to Mrs. Felsam's spared life to be an overreaction, but knowing witches, he stood down.

"Are you alright my dear? What were you doing in there?"

"I was assisting the witches with their spells, Your Majesty. There was no need to be concerned." Said Mrs. Felsam, seemingly sharing the witches' disdain for his melodrama. This embarrassed and upset Jori. His fear for her life was born of genuine concern and care. Perhaps he had misjudged their relationship.

"Would you like to meet them?" Necerta said, offering the slightest hint of a grin as she struggled to contain her self-satisfaction.

"Well, yes… of course!"

Jori turned his attentions to the cave entrance. Three strong men stared back at him. The first of the three approached him and addressed him.

"Your Majesty, it is a pleasure. My name is Edevus. Although we have not met in this form, be safe in the knowledge that we know you, and we have done since we were all in this realm together before." Edevus was tall, slender and handsome. His muscular frame adorned with an elegant red and purple robe.

"You have a name? Oh, my dear boy…" Jori was overcome with emotions once again. He had spent the day preparing himself for this moment, but in truth there was little point. Who could know how to react when greeted by someone so old yet so new? So familiar, yet a complete stranger?

"Yes, we have names. We have had them since we can remember."

"And what are your names?" Jori said, addressing the other two men.

"I am Grimmd, your highness, a true pleasure to make your acquaintance at last. We know you so well and are in awe of your achievements and the prowess that you have shown throughout your life. It has been an honour to share our existence with you." Of the two men that Jori had met so far, Grimmd was the most serpentine. His slim, wormlike body covered with a shimmering ochre cloak, far from the toned muscular frame of his brother Edevus, he was slithery and sly. Jori was taken back by such a torrent of praise, although on reflection, these men knew him better than any. For them to hold him in such high esteem was a great accolade indeed.

"I am Avarico Your Majesty. I share the sentiments of my brothers my lord." A silence followed. *Is that it?* Jori thought. Although he did not require a formal or lengthy address from each man, the abrupt nature of the third heir's words left a noticeable hole that his words should have filled. Breaking the silence, Necerta interrupted.

"Well, that's that done. We can share stories and get to know each other on the way home."

"Yes, I suppose so." Jori said, while staring wistfully at his new sons. Each a true sight to behold and worthy heirs in his mind. Edevus was handsome and polite, Grimmd was charming in his own way and Avarico was strong. Even to look at him, you could sense his power. Not a giant by any means, but his robust, muscular build was plain to see under his large, dark green robes.

As the seven passengers squeezed into Jori and Mrs. Felsam's carriage, Jori looked back at his friend as she stood far back from the rear facing door. "Come along Mrs. Felsam, we have done it… we are going home!"

"Your Majesty. I would like to make a request." She said meekly.

"Of course, my dear… we can discuss it on the way. You have given me heirs Mrs. Felsam, you must know that you have my eternal gratitude. Whatever you ask, I'm sure I shall agree. Now get in." He patted the seat beside him encouragingly.

"I wish to stay here. In the East. I would like to visit family and I have some personal matters to attend to."

"Oh… Oh, really?" Disappointment was painted all over Jori's face. "Well, I suppose that would be ok. How long will you be? Shall I arrange you transport?"

"Not too long Your Majesty, only a week or two. And no, I will find my own way back. I will see you at the castle in no time."

"Well, yes… I suppose that's fine then. But just here? There's nothing here. Can't we take you somewhere?"

"No thank you, Your Majesty. There is a town a few minutes from here and I would quite appreciate the walk, it has been a long day."

"Oh, well very well. I shall see you at the castle then?"

"Yes, your highness."

"No more than two weeks, I will see you are rewarded for your dedication on your return."

"As you wish, Your Majesty. Thank you."

Jori looked back puzzled as Mrs. Felsam waved him and his new companions off on their journey. He turned to marvel proudly upon his new heirs, who had exceeded his expectations, even though he wasn't sure what those were.

By the time he took one final concerned look back to Mrs. Felsam, she was gone.

20

INSIDE THE CAVE

"You're sure this will work?" Stulta was uneasy. For all Necerta's confidence, the truth is that they had never tried a spell of this scale before.

"Of course. We've been through the thing so many times now. If you can't commit to this, then it almost certainly won't work. I'm not having you ruin this."

"Sorry Necerta."

"I don't know why you are so desperate for this Necerta." Said Frigus.

"Because this is our one chance. Our chance for a new life, a better life."

"How do you know it will be better? We know nothing of Jorisham."

"Because no one knows us there. No one knows what we've done."

"Then they won't fear us, not like they do here."

"And that's what you want is it? To be feared and cast out? Living on the outside, surviving in the wild, like animals?"

"At least we get peace. Being left alone is a good thing as far as I'm concerned."

"Well you and your new husband can stay here. You can live a long life of solitude and misery with no one to cast your evil little spells on."

"My evil spells? Don't try and blame this all on me. We were all involved, we all knew what would happen."

"I didn't know." Said Stulta. "I didn't know at all."

"You never do." spiked Frigus. "You could fill a library with books written on all those things that you don't know."

"I know you think I'm stupid, but I'm not. All your plans… all your schemes. None of them would work without me. Necerta, you can make people see anything you want them to. All good and well, but without me to make them believe it, you're nothing more than a circus act. And Frigus, your spells are cruel and your riddles are cunning, but people here know who you are. If we did not cloud their minds, you would be hung from a stake immediately. You treat me like I'm not important, but you're both nothing without me."

"There she goes again." Frigus sneered "Your emotions will be the death of you Stulta. That or your stupidity."

"I'm not stupi…."

"Enough!" Necerta cut them both off sharply. "We are not here to quibble and argue, we are here to change our lives. To gain ultimate power over a kingdom… our Kingdom."

"Not our kingdom. It will belong to our 'husbands'." Frigus did not share Necerta's enthusiasm.

"And who will control them? These men are not fit to rule. They are not even men."

117

"We will control them? Ha! More like they will control us."

"She has a point." Stulta added.

"And what is that? You don't think your powers are strong enough to bend one man to your will? Maybe you are as weak as I thought."

"I don't know how strong my powers will be. All this talk of sharing our powers with these men… what if they turn on us? What if once we are in place, they kill us and keep our powers for themselves?"

"They can't. We give them our powers to make the spell work, and then we feed off that power from them. If they kill us, they will revert to their previous form. They must keep us alive, otherwise they will have a lot of explaining to do. How would you feel if your kings suddenly turned into a giant snake?"

"So that's it? That's our future? Borrowing our powers from these men. Hoping they don't kill us."

"They can't kill us, or they will no longer be men. For goodness' sake Frigus, you're starting to sound like Stulta. I thought that you would understand this by now."

"Hey!" Stulta objected.

"Oh, calm down dear. Do you claim to understand this fully?"

"Well, no, but…"

"Of course not. We don't expect you to." Necerta said smugly. "For the parts that you can't comprehend, you will have to trust us. Trust that we can understand. And in return, you will gain power and influence beyond your wildest dreams."

"That doesn't sound too bad. And I just have to feed off their power?"

"Yes."

"How do they get their power? The power that I will drain?"

"Ah yes. Well, that's the part that we don't know yet."

"Even the great Necerta doesn't know... how encouraging." Said Frigus.

"No one can know. That depends on the personalities and tendencies of our hosts."

"Hosts... heirs... husbands. It seems like too much risk to me."

"I hope mine is nice." Added Stulta.

"You naïve fool... Nice? I don't think you have understood. You don't want him nice; you want him powerful. The more power he gains, the more you gain. Look, we can't keep going over this. We either do it, or we don't. They will be here any minute."

"We're allowed to have concerns Necerta, and we don't answer to you."

"Yes, yes. We're all equal here. So, we're agreed then? Because once we do this... there's no turning back."

The witches nodded firmly "Agreed".

After Jori had eventually agreed to their conditions, the three witches stood inside the cave. They had pretended to barely notice the enormous serpent; an instruction given by Necerta in order to strengthen their position. Now as they stood before it alone, they could finally marvel upon its true power and size. The serpent seemed to appreciate its new audience, slithering up and down the cave.

"Make it quick." Said Mrs. Felsam, startling the witches.

"Ah, you're here. Good. Yes, you're quite right, no time to waste." Replied Necerta.

"But it won't be quick." Added Frigus unnecessarily.

119

"The process won't be quick by any means. We need to amplify the power using the caves, and that takes time to build up. But rest assured that your involvement will be swift, and any discomfort will be momentary."

"Discomfort?" Mrs. Felsam was clearly uneasy.

"Yes, momentary. I can't say how it will feel, but I can say how long it will last."

"And you'll let them go?"

"Why, of course. They will be freed as soon as this is done. We will send our message back west to Laakso the minute we exit this cave."

"You will pay for what you have done."

"Pay? For what? We have helped you. We have given you everything that you asked. We have rescued your family and returned them to their lives."

"In return for my life."

"Of course. That's what you wanted isn't it? to give up your life to save theirs? Or has so much time passed that you forget how you came to us, begging and pleading."

"Yes, but you could have saved them and released them without this. It was within your power."

"But that wasn't the deal was it? You can't change these things in the eleventh hour. What is done is done."

"But it can be undone. They are free, you have saved them. You could let them go from wherever you are keeping them and let me go free as well."

"And why would we do that? We only rescued them in the first place because of what you could offer us. If you are withdrawing your side of the bargain, then we shall withdraw ours."

"And what of the witch that took them? Is she still alive? You haven't even told me how you freed them."

"Rest assured that all is handled. Your family are safe and returned to their land. Although, I would recommend that they move further east where it is safer. The further west you go, the closer they will be to her. And she'll want them back."

"Don't worry. We've made the mistake of heading west before. Now that I shall not return, neither will my loved ones."

"Yes, well… don't dwell on it. What's done is done, and you've got what you wanted."

Witches knew many things, enchantments, illusions, potions and poisons. Even their knowledge of history was broad and deep; they prided themselves on both their knowledge and wisdom. One thing that witches did not know however, was how to comfort a woman who was facing her final few living hours. Mrs. Felsam had never felt so alone, she desperately tried to gain the comfort that she needed from reminding herself of the noble sacrifice that she was making, and that her family were saved.

Frigus sat in the carriage opposite her new 'husband'. She watched as Necerta and Stulta weaved their magic with their twisting, flowing hands. Her thin lips rose into a cruel smirk, as she watched Jori carefully wave goodbye to thin air.

21

HOMECOMING

As they approached the castle's understated rear gates, Jori's excitement turned to worry. So far, Mrs. Felsam's plan had exceeded his every expectation. He was returning home with not one, but three heirs and his legacy was all but secured. He knew he would have a lot of explaining to do as soon as he returned. Even if he had done so alone, he would still have a lengthy absence to explain. His story of collecting a contraption from the North-East would not hold up, given the lack of said contraption and the notable absence of Mrs. Felsam. His tension was visible in the back of the carriage. Until now, the men had been happily acquainting themselves with their father in their new form.

Their eagerness to learn of his ways and receive his wisdom gave him great comfort. Every word that he imparted on them was gratefully received and accepted. This was of great importance to Jori, he had to be sure that they would rule in the same way that he did. He told them of the equilibrium that kept Jorisham together; the balance between work and restitution that kept his subjects happy and allowed the kingdom to thrive. They understood the ethical laws that underpinned his society and agreed wholeheartedly, dispelling any doubts that Jori had held regarding their suitability to rule his kingdom. These men were carved in his own image; the very embodiment of his ideals and beliefs. Jori had felt a fool to doubt them. Witchcraft had always scared him a little, but for him at least, it had always delivered when he needed it most. Here he was, sharing the carriage with the finest three sons that he could imagine... and their wives of course.

Jori's interactions with the witches were limited. They had shared three days together, but his understandable fixation on his new sons had meant that he did not get to know them well; this suited the witches. His relationship had however, improved. Far from the cold abrupt nature of their 'negotiations', the witches were warm and friendly with Jori. He had known not to expect much in the way of affection from their kind, though he had experienced friendship before. Whilst the witches were not excluded from Jori's lengthy discussions with his sons, their input was limited. He occasionally probed them for their opinions, but it was clear that he was doing to with a thinly veiled agenda. More than anything, Jori wanted to understand the ambitions of the witches. He knew as well as any that no matter how strong a man could be, many did not possess the strength to defy their partner. He also knew the strength of a woman, let alone a witch.

As a direct result of Jori's actions, his efforts to found and expand his kingdom were hampered. Almost every single living man who was able to carry a sword had perished at the hands of barbarian monsters. The handful of men that were left were not the strongest and were spread far and wide across the realms. For half a generation, and the most important period the kingdom faced, Jori had needed to rely upon the skill and strength of his female subjects. It was not long until Jori had realised the error of his thinking up until this point, it was only slightly longer until he discovered that he had no real need for men at all.

These formative years for the kingdom shaped the way that it would be ruled thereafter. Women in Jorisham were held in higher esteem than any before them. Having built and formed the industrial sector, cultivated the lands for farming, and physically built the kingdom from nothing, there was no way that Jori's society could face any kind of imbalance. If anything, men were having to prove that they were more than strong oafs capable of lifting heavy objects.

Since the kingdom began, it was the women who held senior positions, with men occupying the lower ranks... except for the army. Despite his efforts to pretend otherwise, this made Jori very proud. He did however, feel less pride with regard to the imbalance within the armed regiments; though he had always consoled himself with the fact that his army was of little to no consequence. Jorisham had only known peace and Jori always knew that he had an ace up his sleeve, so the need for an army was almost non-existent. Instead, the army served as a social structure for the king; he could promote those whose company he enjoyed so that he could spend more time with them. Generals and commanders were always called to the dining hall, with the position carrying great status. This allowed Jori a formal way of selecting his circle of friends without having to do so in an obvious manner. He could drink and relax with his companions, safe in the knowledge that he was among allies.

Jori felt a similar peace and safety among the company of his new sons. Their shared ethics was a relief to him, as was the apparent lack of ambition from their newly acquired wives. After his three days travelling, he felt he had got the measure of the witches quite well. Necerta was fearsome and headstrong, but more than anything he felt that she just wanted love and security. If there was anyone that he knew who could say the right things to assure her of this, it would be Grimmd. Stulta was a simple being, in two ways. Her obvious lack of understanding and speed of thought made her less of a threat. She lacked the foresight for manipulation and the cunning required for subterfuge.

Stulta's ambitions were also simple. Her lack of thought had made her insecure among witches, her relative beauty resulted in her being viewed as 'less of a witch'; a sentiment that neither of her compatriots made any effort to hide. Now she was here, a queen in her own right, she could not be doubted again. She was on her way to acceptance and adoration; not as a witch, but as a queen.

Frigus was more difficult to read. Jori had assumed there was a greater depth to her than he could see, as what he could see was rather lacking; all that he could see is what she lacked. Frigus was a woman without warmth, compassion or tenderness. There was no hint of joy in her eyes. Through frequent moments on their travels, Jori had delivered some of his tried and tested tales and executed his classic punch lines to great effect, as always. His sons guffawed and revelled in his wit and charm, the witches laughed more politely, including Frigus; but her eyes always told a different story. Frigus' eyes were piercing. They were such a light blue that they almost disappeared into the white that surrounded them. Her pupils were forever small, poking and probing into the souls of any who encountered her steely gaze.

Love and security would bring happiness to Necerta, adoration and respect would bring peace to Stulta. 'What...' he thought '...does Frigus seek?'. While this question nagged at him, Jori did not have the time to address it. He had so much to learn and so much to teach, and such little time.

At the gates, Jori's visible apprehension was addressed by Edevus "What's the matter father? Getting nervous?"

"I'm just excited, dear boy. But there is a lot we still need to resolve."

"Resolve?"

"Yes... you see... When I left, I did so under false pretences, and now I will have to explain what really happened. And... I'm not sure I can."

"And your staff are dear to you father, it's important to you to be honest with them." This made Jori glow further.

"That's right. I fear that they will be resistant or suspicious of your arrival."

"But they are *your* staff." Added Avarico brashly. Edevus swung his head towards him, burning him with his gaze.

"It's important that they are respected though brother." Edevus tilted his head towards the old man, who was looking at him quizzically.

"Yes of course. They must be, I just meant that..." stuttered Avarico.

"I think what Avarico was trying to say, father..." soothed Grimmd "...Is that they are your staff and have known and loved you for many years. If you believe that this is the right path, they will surely agree. They may just need time."

"That's right father, that's what I meant. I just didn't put it well." Said Avarico firmly.

"Oh, yes, you are all right I suppose. Maybe they will need time. Maybe we all do." Said Jori with a sigh.

"Quite right, father. I think we should address them all. All together. If we bite the bullet, it will give them more time. I think you may even find that they are more open minded than you think." Edevus cast a sly look to his wife as she stared blankly back at him.

Jori's worries were eased.

As he expected, when he entered the castle door, he was greeted with a flurry of questions.

"Where have you been?"

"Are you well Your Majesty?"

"Are you hungry?"

"Where is Mrs. Felsam?"

"Did everything go well?"

"How are you feeling?"

"Will Mrs. Felsam need feeding?"

"Shall we get the guards to assist with the machinery?"

"Are you cold? You look cold."

Calia said nothing, but ran to him and embraced him warmly. "I'm glad you're back safe Your Majesty." Jori was taken back, as were the other staff, although they did share her sentiment

"All right all right. That's enough of that. I will explain everything… just let me breathe. We shall meet in the main hall in ten minutes."

22

A WARM WELCOME

"Thank you all for coming. Is everyone here?" Jori had adopted his usual stance for this kind of address. His chest was puffed and his legs were wide. Unfortunately, due to his old age and ill health, this did not have the desired effect. Far from the proud cockerel like pose that he was previously able to adopt, he now looked more like a bony marionette puppet, operated by a novice. His chest was high, his arms were limp, his legs unstable beneath him. In stark contrast to the three men towering behind him. Each, the very model of strength and confidence. Beside each man was his wife. Necerta draped herself elegantly beside Grimmd, Frigus stood firmly at the side of Avarico and beside Edevus was Stulta, gently weaving and twisting her hands in front of her, slowly and subtly so that she wouldn't attract attention.

"We are Your Majesty." Replied Mrs. Buxhall, indignation creeping into her voice. "Aside from Mrs.

Felsam…" She raised her eyebrows to punctuate the first of their many unanswered questions.

"Ah yes… Mrs. Felsam." Jori steadied himself. "As some of you may know, Mrs. Felsam came here some years ago from her home in the East. When we were returning, she asked for a leave of absence so that she could head south from where we were and attend to some matters in her home town."

"How long will she be gone for?" asked Mrs. Haughley.

"I'm not sure entirely, but two weeks I should think."

"Can we have two weeks leave Your Majesty" Mrs. Buxhall was now mirroring the King's stance, but with much greater effect.

"No. There is much work to be done. As you may have noticed, we have guests."

"Guests, Your Majesty? It has been some time."

"Yes. Well, not guests entirely. These men will be staying here indefinitely. It is their home."

"Their home, Your Majesty? This is your home. Your home and ours." Said Mrs. Buxhall proudly.

"No, it is also theirs, for these men…" He paused for effect "… are my sons." Jori was prepared for a gasp, some muttering and excited speculation. What followed instead, was silence. Cold, hard, inescapable silence.

"Sons." Said Mrs. Buxhall finally. Not inquisitively but plainly. They knew of his plight; they had been pondering it for two weeks now. They knew the one thing that would resolve their issues immediately. They also knew that this was not in any way possible.

"Yes, I should have said something before, but I didn't know if they would want to come home. It's a lot to take on and I wasn't sure that they would want to come back here.

This is Edevus, Grimmd and Avarico." The men nodded in unison.

"Come home? We've never seen or heard of these 'sons' before."

"Ah yes, well they have been away."

"Away?"

"Yes. During my travels some time ago, I fathered them and they grew up in the North-East."

"So, you 'fathered' these children and then returned home? Leaving them to grow up without a father?"

"Yes, I shall spare you the details, but it was the right thing to do in the circumstances."

"The right thing to do?"

"Are you going to repeat me all day Mrs. Buxhall? You are treading on thin ice here. I am your king, and I am telling you it was the right thing to do." Grimmd slithered next to the king and gently held his shoulder.

"Perhaps I should explain father?"

"OK… do your best. I told you they wouldn't listen." The king huffed and flopped into his chair.

"Good day, wonderful people. We have heard so much of your loyalty and devotion to our father and we are extremely grateful. I understand that this is a very difficult situation to comprehend and to come to terms with, but please allow me to explain." He cast a pleading look at Mrs. Buxhall, who crossed her arms and sat down as well.

"Go on then. We're all ears."

"Our mother was close with King Jori and she held a high position in the North-East. Given the rules that govern our region, a relationship between the two of them would have caused her untold complications. Your king did the right thing by leaving us with our mother, whom he looked after well from afar. Although I appreciate your concern, we did not grow up destitute and fatherless. Far from it. Our mother met a kind man who took us on as his own and raised us happily and well." Grimmd scanned the room to assess how effective his words were. Their eyes had softened and his audience was captured, their eager faces leaning in to hear more. Even Jori was intrigued by his tale, almost forgetting that it was entirely fabricated. He continued. "You all know the love that Jori had for Lowena. Many of you also know that a love that burns as strong as theirs did, cannot be replaced. My mother was a caring woman, but she was equally pragmatic. She knew that no matter how she felt about your king, he could not reciprocate those feelings. Not entirely. But she was not saddened, the sadder thing would have been to ignore her better instincts and deprive us of the happy childhood that we had. Your king and my mother would stay in contact and she would keep him updated with what we were doing. He would send presents for us, and was openly spoken about in our family."

"And the other man? The man who raised you?"

"Oh, Lord Beighton? He was a kind and gentle man. Older than our mother, but a very capable father. He was happy in the situation. In truth, I don't think he could father any children, so this was really the best outcome for all."

"And Jori didn't visit?"

"No. That wouldn't have been right. We had stability, which is important for children. Your king visiting would have disrupted that. This can't have been easy for our father either."

"And why are we just hearing about this now?" Mrs. Buxhall had thawed, but still had a lot of questions.

"Because we had our lives in the North-East, we have wives of our own and our careers. He didn't want to disrupt that and throw us into something that we were not suited for."

"And what changed?"

"Our father came to visit us a few days ago and told us of the situation, and in truth, we couldn't have been happier to assist."

"And why was that? That you were all so happy to leave?" suspicion beginning to rise in Mrs. Buxhall's voice.

"Because we had just moved back home. We had been working in the North-West, giving aid, and helping those in need. I don't know if you have heard, but there are parts of that area that are very poor indeed. We have formed a committee that helps those in such dire need. Our project had come to an end and we were beginning to make new plans. When our father arrived with his proposition, we could not refuse."

"Well... that sounds very noble of you."

"We do what we can Mrs. Buxhall. Father told us countless stories of Lowena and her compassion and her benevolence were a huge inspiration to us."

"Oh, that is good to hear." The room was won over and Jori was as relieved as he was impressed. Buoyed by this, Jori stood up once more and continued his address.

"You will have also noticed my boys' wives, who we are lucky enough to have staying here with them. May I introduce Necerta, Stulta and Frigus. I'm sure that you will come to know each other well over the coming years. I may not know them well, but they are good hearted women, and a true asset to my family. Now, does anyone have any other questions? I remember something about dinner?"

"How will they rule?" Calia had stayed mute up until this point. She had been the most suspicious of all the staff but had decided to keep her head below the crowd. Mrs. Buxhall may be self-appointed, but she was a worthy spokesperson for the castle staff, and always had been. However, her clear newfound adoration for the young men had blunted her otherwise sharp intuition.

"How do you mean dear?"

"Well, there are three of them, and one of you. Are you planning on dividing the kingdom?" Jori did not like Calia's tone. Considering the great defrosting of Mrs. Buxhall, the relative impertinence of Calia was unwelcome.

"My dear, they shall rule by committee."

"After all, three heads are better than one." Charmed Edevus, who was as pleased with his witty retort as those around him. Appreciative smiles filled the room.

"Yes, but shouldn't the throne go to the eldest son? Who is the eldest?"

"Edevus is the oldest." Jori blurted "…then Grimmd, then Avarico." The three men looked at each other slightly bemused. They nodded their heads in agreement, covering their confusion.

"So why does Edevus not take the throne?"

"Because this is the way I have decided it."

"If I may interject, Your Majesty?" Grimmd had slithered forward again. "We were brought up to appreciate the importance of fairness and equality. To rule over a nation like this requires… how shall I put this… balance." The room nodded happily again. "We each bring different skills and knowledge to the task, each able to contribute in ways that the others cannot. By ruling as a group, we will be able to do so in the most balanced and fair way possible."

133

"As a group? So, the three of you, or the six of you?" Calia had locked eyes with Necerta during Grimmd's rebuttal. Necerta was now standing alone, and to Calia, she looked more threatening.

"The three of us. The three rightful heirs. If you are referring to our wives, they will not be involved in the running of the kingdom. They are here for our own support. Nothing more."

"Is that OK with you, child?" Added Jori, showing his dissatisfaction at her line of questioning.

"Of course, Your Majesty. I was just thinking of what the people of the kingdom will ask when this is brought to them, they do not know you as well us we do your highness."

"Hmmm." Jori paused, reassessing his defensive position. "Yes, I suppose that you are correct there. We will have to address the kingdom as we have done here. It seems as though everyone is satisfied with the current situation now?" He cast his tired eyes around the room in search of objection.

"Yes, Your Majesty. Very pleased indeed. It may be unorthodox, but stranger things have happened." Mrs. Buxhall's voice was back to its bouncy rural timbre. "And may I add what a pleasure it is to have you with us."

"The pleasure is all ours." Soothed Edevus. Jori cast a quizzical eye to Calia. She may not have a position of authority within the castle, but it was clear that he respected and appreciated her opinion, as difficult as it may be at times.

"Welcome to the castle your majesties. Your highnesses?" she said. Jori scoured her tone for sarcasm, yet found none. His sons were right; maybe he didn't give his staff enough credit.

23

WORK TO BE DONE

The next few days were a flurry of planning and organising; Jori was in his element. From his days in the council to the time Jori had spent laboriously building his kingdom, one thing was true; Jori thrived when he was busy. Shouting orders, making plans… the castle was a whirlwind of activity, centred around Jori. The last few decades had been slow, and to Jori, boring. These peaceful tranquil years had given him too much time to think, to reminisce and to drink. Jori was back where he wanted to be, but unfortunately, he was no longer who he wanted to be. Despite his drive and determination, all the frantic planning was taking its toll on the old king.

"You need to slow down." Urged Calia gently, as she helped him into his bed. She had come to give him his evening remedies, only to find him hunched over his dresser, struggling to keep himself upright.

"You know I can't slow down, there isn't enough time."

"You'll run out of time faster if you carry on like this."

"You're spending too much time with Mrs. Buxhall, Calia. You don't want to end up like that sour old tyrant."

"HA. I suppose you are right in some way, Your Majesty. Although I wouldn't call Mrs. Buxhall sour."

"Not to her face you wouldn't!" he grinned.

"Not in any way. You know she cares for you and only wants to see you happy and well."

"I am happy dear girl. The happiest I have been in an age. All of this… It's just so exciting."

"It certainly is sir. I just hope it's not *too* exciting."

"No such thing. You can never have *too much* excitement, remember that."

"Any excitement wouldn't go a miss."

"You're overworked dear. But don't worry, things are going to get a lot easier for you once my boys are in charge."

"Easier? How do you mean, Your Majesty?"

"There are going to be some changes around here once I'm… you know."

"You know I don't like you talking like this."

"Come dear, we both know I only have a few days left. We should be able to talk freely of my 'impending demise'."

"Riddles."

"What?"

"I don't like it when you talk in riddles, Your Majesty. If something is to happen to me, I would rather just know now, rather than dread it for days. *Even if it is only a few.*" She gave the old man a wry smile, which he returned.

"Don't worry Calia. That's why I'm so busy. Busy making plans. Plans that will benefit everyone, none more so that you and your brother Viga."

"More riddles."

"Not riddles girl, just things that are not yet set in motion. Surprises, if anything. Not riddles. You need to be more trusting, all will be revealed at my nation address."

"Very well, I won't pry any further. And I do trust you. I'm just not sure I trust them yet."

"Now listen, I know this is all new, but you need to be less resistant to this. They are good people. Good people indeed. I wouldn't be doing all of this if there were not."

"I Know, Your Majesty."

Jori had spent his final days planning. He planned with his sons, he planned with his staff, and there were times when he planned alone. These times were concerning to his new heirs. He locked himself inside his room for hours on end, refusing entry to all, even Viga and Calia. They all knew that he had surprises up his sleeve, yet they could not bear not knowing what they were. Princes, princesses, maids, cleaners, and guards all took turns in lingering outside his door to try to understand what he was busy with. All they could hear was muttering and the occasional angry outburst.

Two days before his national address was due, Jori opened the door to his chambers and fell out, nearly knocking over a statue. He was exhausted and depleted. Whatever he had been doing in that room had seemed to drain his very essence. He was clutching a scroll close to his chest. Calia and Viga helped him to his feet and carried him back to his bed.

"It's OK, Your Majesty. Just take it easy and rest."

"Please Calia, in case I don't make the address. Here is my speech."

"Father!" Bellowed Edevus, rushing to hide side. "What happened? Are you alright?"

137

"He's fine" Said Viga. "He's just tired." Calia mopped his furrowed brow and looked up. The room suddenly felt full, his three sons sharing the same concerned, pitying look.

"Is he OK? What happened?" asked Grimmd.

"He's Fine. He's old and unwell and this has all been too much. It's too much for him." pleaded Calia.

"Yes, of course dear. How may we assist his majesty?"

"You can leave and give him some peace."

"You get to bed father; we will assist you with anything you need tomorrow." Said Grimmd.

"Thank you. Such good boys. I am truly lucky."

"And that? What is that? Can we assist you with that scroll?" Grimmd's eyes gestured towards his hands.

"Oh, yes. I'm glad you're here. I have prepared my speech for the address; in case I am not well enough to deliver it."

"Shall we keep it safe until then, Your Majesty?" he offered.

"Yes, I was rather hoping that you would." He handed the scroll to Grimmd and fell back, as if completing a quest.

"We shall leave you to rest, Your Majesty."

"Thank you by boys... Thank you."

"Get some rest Your Majesty." Calia said, moving her hand on top of his. He placed his other hand on top of hers.

"It is done." He said, directing a smile towards her, then to Viga. "It is finished." Calia knew better than to question his riddles while Jori was in this state. She pulled her hand away and patted his hands.

"Come on Viga. Let us leave, the king needs to rest."

"That had better be *some* speech." Said Viga as they descended the large staircase from his quarters.

"How do you mean?" asked Calia.

"Well, he's been planning for the best part of a week now, frantic meetings and long discussions. Even in his state… But to write a speech that takes that much from him? It had better be worth it."

"If that was what he was doing in there. He's tired and old. I'm surprised that he's lasted as long as he has. I wish they would leave him alone."

"The princes?"

"Yes, they don't give him a moment's peace."

"They have a lot to learn and I would rather they did. I know Jori has warned us of great changes, but I just don't want anything to change. I like things as they are."

"I could do with a change."

"Oh, come on… You've got it made. You are given food, shelter and all that time to ride your horse. You don't get that in other jobs."

"Yes, but it won't be the same. It can't. King Jori is this job. The princes, they all have wives… and I hardly know them."

"Don't worry, they will be old men soon, and I'm sure they will find you charming then. Listening to their stories and tucking them in at night." Calia thumped Viga in the ribs.

"And what will you do? They clearly don't need to be dressed by a simpleton. It's a very specific role you have as well, how long will that last when the Princes become Kings."

"I suspect it will be busier. Three kings need more assistance than one. I imagine that I will be run off my feet." The prospect added a bounce to Viga's step as he hopped down the staircase from Jori's room.

139

"The more errands you run, the more errors you make, Viga. How sympathetic will your new kings be then?" Viga stopped in his tracks. "I didn't mean it like that. I just mean that it will be a change for all of us. How will I get away with so much time off with Astrus? How will they tolerate it when Mrs. Buxhall speaks out of turn? Or when Mrs. Haughley scolds them for not finishing their food? We all have a lot of change coming our way."

"Yes, but like Jori says… There will be good changes for us."

"You said it yourself, change isn't often good."

"I'm not sure that what I said, or meant. Maybe I will be made a general of the army. General Viga. I would accept captain even… Captain Viga has a ring to it."

"You, in charge of a hundred men in battle. Goodness help us all."

24

THE SCROLL

My Dear citizens of Jorisham… I come to you with sad news. Sad… but inevitable news. I have been your king for many, many happy years. But now, my time is at an end.

-Pause for sadness to die down-

Yes, I know that this is a sad time. Our long and happy history together has reached its final act. But there is now a new story to be written. I come to you today, to lead you forward into your next journey as a kingdom, a journey that I will not be accompanying you on.

I will however be leaving you in more than capable hands.

As a king… as your king, I am entitled to the privilege of privacy. And in truth, I have hidden some things from you, and my people. I have done so for the welfare and wellbeing of my children, and by that, I mean you loyal people, whom I view as children. But also, my true children.

-Pause for Shock to dissipate-

Yes, that is correct… Standing beside my here are my three sons and heirs to the throne. Their names are Edevus, Grimmd and Avarico. They have travelled from their maternal home to take up their rightful place and true calling as your kings.

Although they were not raised within the kingdom, you will never meet three men with so much of Jorisham running through their veins. They are the human embodiment of all that it great and true of our wonderful kingdom. The compassion and balance that are the cornerstones of our great society will continue to be upheld by these able men. Their hearts are pure, and their intentions noble. You can rest assured that I would not abdicate to these three men, if it were not the absolute correct decision.

Accompanying your new Kings are their wives, Stulta, Necerta and Frigus. Three of the kindest and wisest queens that a kingdom could ask for. Now, I would like to ask any of you if there are any questions that you have? Please raise your hand and someone will come and relay your question to me.

- Answer five questions. Ten at most. Offer to respond in writing if they are not satisfied -

Thank you.

I will hand you over to your new kings shortly, but first I have some matters to deal with, and some good news to share.

-Pause for effect. Look at Mrs. Buxhall and Mrs. Haughley in the crowd. -

My Abdication comes with several conditions, involving the running of both my kingdom and my castle. Firstly, the castle. As many of you know, this castle is family to me. These people have served me well, and with this new era, comes new opportunities for them. I would like to publicly thank four of my closest and oldest staff members and offer them a new life.

Firstly, the fearsome, yet kind cooks, Mrs. Buxhall and Mrs. Haughley. Your services and loyalty to me are beyond praise. I cannot thank you enough for devoting your life in service to me, and I hope that you will accept my gifts in return for this. I have arranged a profitable small holding for each of you, just outside the city walls, where you can both see out your days in peace and security as neighbours.

-Wait for applause to end. Find Viga-

My Dear Viga, always beside my side for the best part of your life. You are humble and brave, if also occasionally clumsy. To reward you for your endless devotion, I have set aside a small castle to the North of Jorisham, where you can create your own life. And what castle would be complete without a title... Lord Viga.

- Find Calia. Hush Crowd-

Calia. Headstrong and kind. I shall miss you most of all. Your kind heart has been wasted on me all these years. It's time to put it to use. For you, there is Heiligdom, a farm on the edge of the City full of animals needing your attention. There is food, there is security and there is a lot of land to ride on. I hope you will find happiness here, and you can build yourself the future you Deserve.

- Wait for applause. Regain composure. Check for tears. Find Mrs Felsam-

Mrs. Felsam, for reuniting me with my dear children, I wish to grant you a business. There is a bakery on Cannon Street which I have purchased in your name. I gift this to you on behalf of the kingdom, which is forever in your debt.

- Address the crowd broadly-

To the rest of my staff who are still able, you will have a job to do… three times the size. From this day on, all castle staff will receive an increase in pay that reflects this tripling of duties.

- Wait for applause -

And now all of you. To all of you loyal, wonderful people whom I have been lucky enough to call my subjects. I gift to you, my Kingdom.

-Pause for gasps, hush crowd-

We have built this Kingdom from nothing, in a time where hope was as scarce as the resources that surrounded us. I know, better than any, that this kingdom would be nothing without its subjects, and in truth, it belongs to all of us.

It is because of this, that I am abdicating my throne to my three sons. To rule in equal measure... but not alone. My years as a king have taught me many things. The most important of these is that power can be too much of a burden for one man to bear, even the strongest man... even three of the strongest men.

To reassure you that this incredible kingdom shall carry on in the same direction that is has been, you will all be involved in the management of it. You shall appoint representatives annually who will share the rule of the kingdom with the Kings. No one person will hold enough power to become blinded by it. Each of you will be the eyes and ears that will inform the beating heart of the kingdom, and together, you will ensure the happiness of all others around you.

- Hold up hands and wait for applause. Thank them for praise. -

Now it is time for me to hand you over to your new Kings, Edevus the wise, Grimmd the noble and Avarico the strong.

25

THE KING'S FINAL DAY

Their laughter filled the room.

Edevus' quarters were the largest of the three brothers', they were also the highest. Secluded at the top of the castle above a long winding staircase. The quarters were originally built for Jori, but he never felt comfortable being so high. He would joke that it was due to his diminutive stature, but in truth it was due to the turmoil he felt regarding his position. Jori was always happy to be a king, he enjoyed the position entirely, but there was always a feeling of being an impostor. He was a noticeably simple man, with simple tastes and inside he felt no different from the subjects who served him. He shared common interests and values with farmers and workers, values which he did not share with fellow leaders or dignitaries. Perhaps that was why he had filled the upper echelons of his society with common soldiers, promoted above their station. Perhaps it is also why he made such a beloved king.

The affinity that he shared with the common man was reciprocated. More than any ruler in his position, his subjects truly believed that he understood their plight. His aversion to the finer things that being a king offered was a way of him remembering this... of remembering who he was and where he came from.

Edevus did not share such an inner conflict. Having landed into power barely two weeks after being cast in human form, Edevus thought that the life suited him well... and that he suited *it*. His new wife Stulta shared his appreciation of their new surroundings, finding herself where she had always wanted to be... above all others. She had filled their new sanctuary with ornate decorations and the room was draped elaborately in the finest cloth that she could find.

Now, on the eve of their inauguration, the kings and witches faced their greatest challenge yet... one that they did not seem to be too concerned with.

"He really thinks that we would accept this? After we've come this far?" Necerta was draped over a dressing table, seductively holding her glass of wine.

"He's more of a fool than we thought." Slithered Grimmd. "And fools are easily fooled."

"Yes, I'm with you on that Grimmd. We can't let this be delivered. I say we leave this to the women to resolve." Said Edevus.

"How gracious Your Majesty." Mumbled Frigus.

"And by women, I meant the useful ones, Frigus." Edevus grinned charmingly at her.

"Oh, I have my uses. You will see just how useful I can be."

"Ok, calm down, I was only teasing. I don't want to witness your powers, 'sister'. I only meant that this is a job more suited to the others."

"Yes, a perfect solution if you ask me." Added Grimmd. "Necerta, my beloved… Without any disrespect intended, are you capable of creating such a big illusion?" Necerta raised a sharp eyebrow. He continued. "We have seen the effectiveness of your powers at the cave, and they are very impressive. But that was one man, who *wanted* to believe your trick. What we're talking about now is an entire kingdom."

"Don't you worry dear husband; I will not be working alone." She cast a knowing glance to Stulta. "Creating an illusion is one thing, but believing it is another. That's what has kept us together all these years." She smiled at Stulta and began to pace the room. "I can make people see anything they want to see." her body twisted and swirled until she took the form of Stulta "But people need to do more than just see. They need to believe." She reverted from Stulta's form, much to the relief of the real Stulta and took the form of King Jori. "For Jori, it was easy. Like you say, he wanted to believe that Mrs. Felsam was alive and well, to relieve him of his own guilt. It is much harder to convince someone of something they do not wish to believe."

"And that's what I do." Interrupted Stulta.

"Quiet! I'm telling a story." Said Necerta sternly, as she continued to slither around the room, slaloming between the three brothers. Stulta sulked back into her chair. "So, we will agree to your plan, dear Edevus. I shall cast the illusion, and Stulta will make them believe it, just as she did with Jori's words to his staff. But you are correct husband, we will need more power."

"More power? So, it is true? You can't do this alone?" Grimmd seemed excited at the possibility of weakness in his wife. Her growing confidence since she arrived in the capital had begun to make him feel uneasy.

"Not exactly. For we are not alone… we have you." The men looked cautiously at each other. "We are bound together, each of us. Me to Grimmd, Stulta to Edevus and Frigus to Avarico. Your power gives us strength."

"Our power?" Said Avarico with a frown.

"Yes. You are powerful men your highness. And you need to stay powerful. We all do."

"And what if we don't?" Avarico's tone was becoming increasingly sinister.

"Then you will go back to where you came from, or rather… what you came from."

"So, we must stay in power, to keep your strength and keep us in this form? I don't remember agreeing to this."

"I don't remember you agreeing to anything. All I remember is you cowering in the shadows for decades until your master wanted something from you." Frigus revelled in the position of power the witches had found themselves in. The other witches rolled their eyes.

"Well, we are here now, and we won't be pushed around by the likes of you three." Said Edevus.

"We don't intend to push you around; we just need you to know the balance that we are all faced with. It's in all of our interests to stay powerful, alive and in… human form." Said Necerta, as the faintest grin crept into the corners of her thin mouth. "We are all in the same position, standing precariously on the same sheet of ice. One wrong move could see us all perish. We need to work together."

"Well, we can't argue with that my dear. We must all stand united in our rule. We all want the same things, yes?" said Grimmd.

"Of course, Grimmd." Beamed Stulta, seemingly relieved that the argument was over. "One big happy family."

"Indeed." Said Grimmd warmly. "So, what do you need of us to increase you power enough to execute this illusion?"

"You will see."

That evening, Jori called a staff meeting in his quarters. Mrs. Buxhall, Mrs. Haughley, Calia and Viga huddled around his bed awkwardly.

"So, here we all are. I just wanted to thank you all for all that you have done for me in the last few weeks. It really has been an extraordinary time, and one that I am grateful to have shared with you all. After my abdication speech tomorrow, we will need to make arrangements for what happens in the castle afterwards."

"Arrangements?" asked Mrs. Buxhall.

"Yes. With the changes that we will see, there will be three new kings in charge of this castle, as well as the rest of the kingdom. From tomorrow onward, this will be their home. It would not be right for me to stay here and loiter around like a bad smell, a ghost haunting the corridors. No… I have made arrangements for a nice cottage in the city where I can see out my final days."

"A cottage? For a king?" Mrs. Buxhall asked with a hint of outrage.

"Not for a king. For an old man who has earned some peace and quiet."

"Well, who will look after you?"

"Like I said, I have made arrangements. There is a cook and a nurse, they will look after me. As for you, I would hope that you would visit me."

"Visit?" said Calia "I'll do more than visit; I would stay with you and look after you. This 'nurse' of yours is a stranger, who is she to help you in your…"

"…Final few days? Dear girl, please do not think me too old and frail to make my own decisions. Besides, I can guarantee that as of tomorrow, you will all be too busy with your own lives to have the time to dedicate to serving me. No, those days have passed." Calia huffed and cast an expression that Jori had seen many times before. "Do not sulk. It will all be fine, and it is what I wish. Now, please can you make the travel arrangements for tomorrow? And most of all, please do not share this information. I want peace and quiet, not an entire kingdom of well-wishers in and out of my door all hours of the day."

"As you wish, Your Majesty." Said Mrs. Buxhall, looking firmly at Calia.

"Of course, Your Majesty." Said Calia.

"Right, well that's that sorted. Now if you are all satisfied, please leave me to get some sleep. Tomorrow is a big day for us all. A big day for the whole kingdom!" he grinned happily and sank back into his pillows.

26

A BIG DAY

Jori had always been an early riser. On the morning of one of the most important days he could recall, he did so with great excitement. Despite his early schedule, he would often be greeted by Viga or Calia as he rose, ready to assist him with wherever he needed it. This morning he woke much earlier than usual, understandably so, given the gravity of the day that lay ahead. When he opened his eyes, it was not Viga looking back at him, nor Calia… but Frigus.

Frigus' presence could suck the warmth out of the liveliest room. Her sharp, angular face was twisted into a semi-sympathetic smile, her eyes told another story. "Good morning, Your Majesty." Jori froze, he was confused and unnerved.

"Err… good morning dear. Why are you…"

"I just wanted to apologise Your Majesty."

"Apologise?"

"Yes. I fear that I have not been as open with you as I should have liked, and that I do not share the bond that you do with Necerta and Stulta."

"Well, I wouldn't say we have a bond, but they are nice young women. And the boys seem to like them."

"And I am not a nice young woman?" Frigus' smile began to slip.

"No, I didn't mean that. I just... It's very early and I haven't got my head straight yet." Jori sat up and repositioned himself. He rubbed his eyes in order to illustrate his point, sighed and continued. "I suppose you are right. We haven't found a closeness, but there is still time. I'm only abdicating today, I will have more time after this is all over to get to know you better." Frigus doubled her efforts at softening her expression, stretching out her smile and reaching out to hold his hand.

"Oh, I do hope so." She said, her smile bordering on a grimace. "I never knew my father growing up, he was a cold, hard man with little emotion. I suppose that's why I'm like this."

"Like what?" said Jori, with genuine concern and care.

"I struggle to make friends, to form attachments. I haven't always been this way, only since life became more serious for me."

"More serious?" Jori leaned forwards. He may not have prepared himself for such an unexpected guest, but he could not have prepared himself for her to open up to him in this manner.

"Yes, the East. It's not an easy place. Killed or be killed... that kind of thing. I suppose that when life got tough, I survived by becoming tougher. And when life became hard, cold and difficult... so did I."

"Dear child, you do not need to worry. We all do what we can in this life. You needn't beat yourself up about it. And look… look where you are now. Living in a castle as a queen. Life is no longer hard for you. Give yourself time and you will be how you used to… if you allow yourself." Jori was pleased with that. He had only just woken up, far earlier than usual, but had managed to deliver some of his more profound advice to someone who had seemed to really need it. Even this late in his life, Jori was making the kind of difference that he had striven to make, ever since Lowena had passed. It may not have been the start to the day that he had expected, but it was one that he appreciated.

"Thank you, Your Majesty, such kind and wise advice."

"You are welcome my dear. Now, please fetch Viga if you will, I would like to get up and prepared."

"Of course, Your Majesty. And one more thing if I may…"

"Yes dear?" Frigus held Jori's had tight with both hands and looked deep into his eyes.

"Today will be a long day for you, it will be very tiring. You must look after yourself. It would be terrible if the strain of today were to hasten your passing in any way. You wouldn't want to pass away before you can start your new life." A cold shiver ran down Jori's spine, he withdrew his hands from under hers.

"Yes… well… don't you worry about that. I still have plenty of fight left in me." He retreated up the bed into his pillows, clearly perturbed by her odd words.

"Absolutely Your Majesty… that's the spirit." Frigus' smile was broader and more genuine than it had been at any point during their awkward emotional exchange. She patted his leg and took her leave.

***

Jorisham was founded on the principle of fairness. This could be seen throughout the entire Kingdom, from the treatment of workers in the centre of the city, to the rules that governed the outlying farms. Jorisham was built on agriculture, the fertile lands and hardworking farmers provided the kingdom with ample resources and tradable goods that allowed it to grow and thrive. King Jori knew this well and even though the city had grown beyond its simple farming beginnings, the farming lands that surrounded the city were respected and protected by law.

To ensure fairness and equality across these farm lands, Jori had established 'The Central Crop Trust'; an organisation that collected all crops grown by farmers and delivered the profits back to them, with a minimum fee issued. The trust would then divide up the crops and distribute them to be sold inside the city and exported to other kingdoms. This system worked well for the farmers, guaranteeing them a minimum return on their harvest and protecting them from the insecurity that comes from this line of work.

It was now almost harvest time in Jorisham, when the central crop convoy would roll through the villages, collecting crops and delivering the money from the previous month's harvest. This month however, the convoy was larger than usual; there were large open wagons for collecting crops, but also armoured carriages escorting them. The farmers and villagers had never seen anything like this. King Jori's military had seldom needed to venture out of the city walls, let alone grace the outlying farms with their presence. The simple dwellings that surrounded the farms were a flurry of excitement. Children eagerly lined the muddy roads leading into the homesteads and every labourer had downed tools in order to behold the spectacle that had visited them. These homesteads existed in a forgotten time, long before Jorisham had been created. They existed as they always had, before the barbarians had invaded. The only changes they saw since King Jori had worked his similar lands were the tools that they used. In Jori's time, the land was worked by ox, horse and man alone. Now, they had basic yet effective machinery courtesy of Jori's connections with the leaders from the North-East. A portion of their profit from the Crop trust was withheld for the purchase and maintenance of these technological advancements, so it was always kept in good working order.

As the convoy approached the head farmers cottage in the centre of the first homestead, the villagers had excitedly surrounded the carriages; eager to witness the reason for such a heavy military presence in their humble home. Janous, the head farmer, was a large man; tall, but with a hard, bulbous stomach that protruded out from him as if he were with child. His complexion was troubled, his cheeks so far past rosy that they looked angry and sore. His messy grey beard and bald red head were a confusing and intimidating site. Janous' voice only had one setting... loud.

"What's all this about then?" he bellowed directly into the face of Mr. Chilton, the crop collector; a meek accountant who had spent his whole adult life travelling from farm to farm collecting crop and reimbursing with coin. Over the years, the men had grown to know each other well; well enough for him to know better than to show Janous any kind of dishonesty or lack of haste.

"There are some changes." He said, his eyes looking up sheepishly. He slumped his shoulders forwards apologetically and he turned his head towards the imposing presence of armed guards.

"What kind of changes?" He shouted, his weather-beaten face growing impossibly more red.

"There are to be new rulers in the kingdom. They are going to change the way that crops are collected."

"More levies I suppose? Well… it won't do. If there are to be any alterations to the way the crop trust operates, then I want to hear it from King Jori. I want to hear his intentions. We are valid members of the trust here and we shall be heard." He projected his voice theatrically to the back of the crowd and raised his arms for endorsement from his employees… which they duly delivered. Once the shouting and clapping had died down, Mr. Chilton approached Janous cautiously.

"I'm sorry Janous. This is extremely difficult for me, and I'm not sure how to say it."

"Just spit it out, coward. How much more are they taking from us and when will they start? We have our biggest crop of the season, if the hikes are too much, we will struggle to pay for what we need the rest of the year."

"I understand that, I do. Please don't think that I had a hand in this. If there was anything I could do, I would."

"A hand in what? Just tell me how much they are withholding now. If it's more than two in ten, I will go and see King Jori myself."

"Please don't make a scene Janous, it will not end well."

"I am not 'making a scene', Mr. Chilton. I am simply trying to get an answer. You come in here, armed to the teeth, delivering news, talking of changes. Well… Go on… How much?"

"All of it."

"All of it?" Janous' aggressive stance had slipped into confused panic. "No, that's not right. That's not how this works. We need that money. We need it for all the things that we can't grow ourselves. We need it for clothes, for medicine. We… we need it for our children. We need it for materials."

"I'm so sorry Janous."

"Sorry? You will be. No, I'm not having this. I refuse. This is not the way of the Central Crop Trust."

"It is now." Called a voice from inside the carriage. A slender man in a dark cloak emerged from the second armed carriage, he was holding a scroll. "I have here, a royal decree that outlines the changes that are forthcoming. I'm afraid the old ways of the trust are over. It is time for a new age of prosperity.

"Well, I refuse. It's not happening. I demand an audience with King Jori."

"To refuse a royal decree… Is treason."

"Ha. Treason? I know the king. I need to speak with *him*."

"…and treason… is punishable by death." The man grinned as two guards grabbed the large man and restrained him. Janous looked pleadingly at Mr. Chilton, who could only shrug.

"I'm sorry Janous, this is the way now. Please don't fight it. I'm sure this can be resolved, just don't do anything rash." Mr. Chilton looked cautiously at the cloaked man and retreated apologetically.

"So, what will it be?" Said the man, addressing the crowd as much as Janous. By this point the confused crowd were being held back by a line of guards. "Compliance?" He paused "...Or treason?" the guards dropped Janous to his knees and the man looked down at him, his sinister grin peeking out from under his hood. Janous looked at the crowd, who could offer no assistance, the armed guards holding them back with ease. He looked for Mr. Chilton, but he was nowhere to be seen.

"You can't do this!" He shouted. "Who do you think you are?"

"What... Will... It... Be?" Said the man, savouring each word. "Do you accept the King's new terms?"

"I can't. We can't. We will starve."

"So be it." He looked at the guards and signalled to Janous. With one quick movement, the guard on the right drew his sword and slit the throat of the large farmer. "Mr. Chilton? Teach these simpletons the new way of things. If they resist, deal with their treason accordingly." With that, he slithered back into his cabin.

"How do you feel?" Said the woman sitting next to him.

"Alive. I feel alive."

"And strong?"

"I have never felt stronger."

"Good. This is what I was trying to explain." She said, and she tightly gripped his hand with hers. Their eyes met, and for the first time since their unconventional union, they shared a spark of love.

"I want to do the next one."

"I thought you might. We'll have to wait for them to clear this up though."

It was only after he felt the life slip out of the old man in the next farm, as he held him in his arms, that Grimmd knew the true nature of the power that Necerta spoke of. As he looked deep into the farmers eyes, his anguish filled him with a glowing satisfaction. He could feel his power growing and swirling inside him. Like many feelings though, this was fleeting. After returning to his wife inside the carriage, he could feel his new sense of gratification slipping away from him. "This feeling, why doesn't it last?" He asked his wife.

"It never can, it has to be absorbed. Enjoy it while you can, dear husband. And don't let it consume you."

"Don't worry, I am stronger than that." He put his hand on her knee as they continued their journey.

As the convoy slowly marched through the countryside, it left a devastation in its wake unseen since the times of the invading hoards so many years ago. Farms were turned to camps, farmers to slaves. Guards were left in every homestead they converted, in order to keep the workers in line. As they tore through the simple, peaceful lands, Grimmd grew in confidence and hunger. His speeches to the farmers grew more elaborate as he broke the news of their new lives with glee.

"Simple folk, for too long have you been reliant on the aid of the city. Today, I grant you freedom, and Independence. No man who has land to tend, food to eat and a home to live in could be considered poor. No. You, *honest* people are the wealthiest among any in the kingdom. I envy you. Today marks the first day of a new life, and a new way of things. Embrace it, I urge you. Accept it, and there you will find peace. There… you will find happiness."

His poisonous words, so full of treachery and deceit, filled him with a lasting and satiating pleasure. As their

160

journey continued, the repetitiveness started to detract from his satisfaction. Each life that slipped away before his eyes grew less and less significant, his only gratification coming from the heart-breaking wails of the farmer's families.

As the day progressed, Grimmd moved from his role at the centre of the villager's anguish to the side-lines. As his men carried out his merciless and cold-blooded slaughter, Grimmd gave comfort to those around him. Holding the wives of the slain farm leaders, he would offer them words of comfort and hush their anguished cries. Necerta looked on, proud of her husband. *He is learning*, she thought. As his power grew, so did hers. Each village filling her with the strength that she needed to perform her greatest feat yet.

Having collected the harvested crops from the farms outside of the kingdom, Grimmd had returned with both crop, and coin. With the money that was due to the farmers, Avarico had purchased even more produce from their neighbouring towns and cities. Grimmd had accompanied him to plead for sympathy from their neighbours. Tales of blight and famine ensured them the compassion they needed to maximise their returns. After their return, the crop reserves of the city were overflowing and kept under constant guard.

27

THE ABDICATION

Jori felt strong and confident, but he could tell that his staff did not share the optimism that he had in his health. Over the past few weeks, everyone inside the castle had become preoccupied with Jori's imminent departure. Conversations within the castle walls had turned from 'what is going to happen to Jori' to 'what is going to happen to the kingdom'. Though the return of his prodigal sons may have answered the questions surrounding the future of the kingdom, it was still unclear what would happen to Jori.

Jori's staff had witnessed his health ebb and flow, with brave rally followed by sombre relapse, his prognosis changed daily. Despite Jori outlining his retirement plans to them the day before, there remained little hope over how long this time of relaxation would last for him. Given his frail, depleted state upon finishing his speech, to the staff, the outlook looked bleak.

Jori did not share their pessimism. Having found solutions to all his issues over the past few weeks, he felt a surge of excitement swirling within him; today was the last day of his rule, but the first of the rest of his life. At no point during his reign had Jori considered another vocation, or indeed a retirement. The length of his life and his abundance of energy had left him with the feeling that he could carry on forever, as a result he had never considered any other option. Now, faced with his evident mortality, he had taken stock of his options for the first time in his life and retirement was a fascinating prospect. He would be allowed all the time to do the things that he enjoyed, without any of the hard work. Hard work had delivered Jori the life that he enjoyed and, in his mind, entitled him to the most peaceful and fulfilling retirement that anyone could wish for.

Of course, Jori knew that he was in his final chapter. At times in the last few weeks, it had seemed like his remaining life could be measured in days, not years. But now, on the eve of his new beginning, Jori had that feeling creeping over him again, that he could carry on like this forever, peacefully and happily. He understood the concern of his staff. Only two days ago, they had witnessed him clinging on to life as he delivered his final speech. What else could they think? Their concern for him frustrated Jori. He knew why they were worried for his health, given what they had seen… who wouldn't be? He only wished that he could explain why, to explain to them what he had been doing to leave him in such a frail state, but this was not the time.

Despite the previous relapses, Jori felt rejuvenated. He was ready for his address and the adoration that it would bring. More than this, he was ready for his new life.

He swelled with pride as he looked down upon his subjects, his three sons behind him; strong pillars, upholding all that he believed in. If he was able to have conceived such a situation, there wouldn't have been a more perfect outcome that he could imagine. As he looked out over the ocean of subjects below him, he was reassured in his conviction... *this feels right.*

Calia and Viga stood anxiously behind the stout but powerful Mrs. Buxhall and Mrs. Haughley. They were not quite sure why they were instructed to observe the speech with the rest of the kingdom, but by this stage they had long since stopped trying to decipher their king's riddles.

Looking up at him, it was hard for them to imagine the frail old man they saw falling out of his quarters only two day before. He may have looked older than any of his subjects had seen him before, but to his staff, the man they knew as king had returned. Behind him stood his three sons, and behind them, their wives. As King Jori began his last speech, Calia gripped Viga's hand tightly.

"My Dear citizens of Jorisham. I come to you with sad news. Sad, but inevitable news. I have been your king for many, many happy years. But now, my time is at an end..."

Waves of shock and confusion rippled through the crowd and a sense of excitement was growing. When Calia had been made aware of the existence of the kings' heirs, it was in a safe space where questions were welcomed and answered willingly. Considering the nature of the announcement, she was unsure why she didn't have more questions at the time. Now, surrounded by the entire Kingdom as the waning king explained his abdication, she was full of more questions than ever before. The murmurings of the crowd made her tingle.

Inside the castle, she had only Mrs. Buxhall to rely on to probe the king for explanations, possibly Mrs. Haughley if she got upset enough… which was rare. Out here in the vast courtyard of the castle, with wave after wave of people flowing into the streets surrounding it, there would surely be too many questions for The King and his sons to deflect so easily. Given that she and the staff had already been told about the arrival of the new kings, Jori's speech was beginning to drag, furthered only by her anticipation of the backlash that was heading to Jori and his sons. She did not wish such a tirade upon her beloved king, especially in this state, but he had been so cryptic in the last few weeks that she was hoping that someone would squeeze a straight answer from him, and it wouldn't be her.

"…Now, I would like to ask any of you if there are any questions that you have? Please raise your hand and someone will come and relay your question to me."

Calia's grip on Viga's hand intensified as she vibrated with nervous excitement, spurred on by the sheer size of the crowd surrounding her. She looked around, but saw nothing. She could see The King, towering over them on his balcony, but could not see any of the crowd. Calia was not tall by any means, but she had never felt so short. She exchanged frustrated looks with both Mrs. Buxhall and Mrs. Haughley, each of whom only just passed five feet tall. They looked up at Viga hopefully, who was staring into the distance across the crowd. "Well?" asked Calia, pulling on his arm.

"Well what?" he replied blankly.

"Has anyone raised a hand? What are they saying?"

"Oh, I hadn't checked." The three short women huffed in unison and rolled their eyes.

"WELL?"

"Nope. It doesn't look like anyone is coming forward, although I can't see much." Calia grunted angrily.

"How can no one have any questions?"

"Well, it's all been explained my dear." Said Mrs. Haughley calmly.

"To us maybe, but not to them. It still makes little sense."

"I think perhaps dear… that the general population are not so emotionally attached to King Jori as you are… as we are… and that they might be a bit more open minded."

"A bit more 'empty minded' more like." snarked Mrs. Buxhall who had never liked the outside world and was sure that the inhabitants of it were depraved lunatics. Mrs. Buxhall's institutionalisation was a constant source of amusement for Calia and Viga, who would often ask her for tales of the world outside the castle walls, only to be spun fanciful yarns and sordid tales of ignorance and immorality.

"Ah, yes Mrs. Buxhall, I forget where we are. Surrounded by 'the great unwashed'. Maybe we will meet some of the characters from your stories? 'The thieving milkmaid'? Perhaps 'the old lady in the woods'?" The thought made Calia laugh, but not unkindly.

"Not the old lady, please." Said Viga, pretending to yawn.

"Hah, are you still scared of her, little brother?"

"No, I'm not scared, I was never scared of her."

"Well, you should be, or she'll turn you to stone!"

"Stop that, both of you. If you knew what I knew, you wouldn't be joking like that, I can tell you."

"Of course, Mrs. Buxhall. Your knowledge of the world never ceases to amaze me, especially considering how often you leave the castle." Said Viga with a wry smile.

"There are more ways of knowing than to see, young Viga. That I can tell you." Calia and Viga rolled their eyes.

"SHHHH!" Said a tall man in front of them. "He's talking." The four looked up at their King, awaiting the changes that they had been anticipating so eagerly.

"I will hand you over to your new Kings shortly, but first I wanted to say a little about the men who will soon be your kings. These three men that stand before you not only embody everything that I stand for, but they go far beyond."

"Jorisham is a society built on compassion and balance. Before I approached them to take their rightful places at the head of this kingdom, these three wonderful men had been travelling the five realms giving assistance to those most in need, dedicating their lives to making this world a better place. Now, we are lucky to have them with us, helping our kingdom be the best that it can be. I may have built this kingdom, but your new kings will lead it into a new age… but they can't do it alone. They will need help."

"As you may know, I have a small number of staff that work for me within the castle. They are down among you today and I wanted to give them the most public of tributes. Mrs. Buxhall, Mrs. Haughley, Calia and Viga. My gratitude for your assistance is both vast and endless. The years of devotion that you and your families have given me shall be long remembered as a service not only to your king, but the whole kingdom. I wanted to thank you today in front of all these people so that they too, could offer their appreciation."

He paused, allowing a torrent of applause to rain down on the four unsuspecting guests. Calia was mortified. She was never one for the spotlight, happy to stay out of sight and do whatever was needed. The sudden attention and applause made her sick to her stomach. Their smiling, genuine faces taunted and tormented her, she wanted to run. Viga on the other hand seemed to enjoy the praise. Viga was not an exceptional member of staff by any means, so to be recognised as such by the entire kingdom filled him with great pride. Mrs. Buxhall fanned her face and made her best effort to appear graceful and dignified, a difficult task for a lady of her stature; her opinion of the general public having seemingly changed somewhat for this instant. Mrs. Haughley turned crimson red and appeared to be attempting to hide her head inside her body like a tortoise, the effect of which made her look like an angry boil. The king did not seem to notice the discomfort of his staff among the masses and continued.

"Your service to me within the castle has made me able to rule in way that I have for all these years. I could not imagine a castle without the four of you in it, and I would wish for nothing more for my heirs than for you to carry on with your duties in service to them. My one last wish as king is that you do not abandon your posts for fear of change, but steady the ship in my absence and help your new kings to rule, as you did for me." Calia's heart sunk. "This is the change he was talking about? THIS?" she fumed.

"It's OK Calia, if the king was so confident that this change will be good for us, then you should trust him." Mrs. Haughley had recovered her head from her neck and placed her hand on Calia's shoulder.

"Trust him? He's lost his mind!"

"Now... *will* you calm down?" Mrs. Buxhall was clearly flustered. "I don't know what you were expecting. This job is as good as it's likely to get and you're lucky to still have it. You're safe in your job and inside the castle."

"Safe." Calia echoed.

"Yes, not everyone can be so lucky. You've got a good job and will keep it for a long time. What more do you ask?"

"Something exciting. The good changes he was talking about. This isn't change, this is the same thing... forever."

"Trust me dear, things will change. These new kings could be the making of you."

Calia said nothing, crossed her arms and continued to sulk.

"... Now it is time for me to hand you over to your new Kings, Edevus the wise, Grimmd the noble and Avarico the strong."

Calia Rolled her eyes and pushed her way through the crowd. She barged her way through the alleyways filled with people, the voices of the new kings getting fainter; the rapturous applause and sycophantic laughter of the crowd deafening to her now. As she broke free from the crowd and made her way to the castle, she was stopped by a guard.

"Hold it. Where are you going?" He said, looking down at her.

"Where am I going? I'm going home."

"Not now you're not. It's not finished."

"Finished? I don't care if it's finished. I live here and I want to go home, let me past."

"I'm afraid I can't do that, young lady."

"Young lady? Do you even know who I am?" she shuddered at the words as she spoke them.

"You are not a King, or a queen. That's all I need to know."

"I am Calia, the kings, well... Maid I suppose. Anyway, I live and work here."

"That may be true miss, but I am not to let anyone out of the area until the speeches are over."

"And why is that? You can't force us to listen to this nonsense."

"Nonsense, young lady? I would be careful if I were you."

"Me, be careful? You need to be careful. When King Jori finds out about this, he'll have your head."

"King Jori?" He said with a smirk.

"You know what I mean. When he hears that you've been stopping me from going to my home, you'll lose your job at the very least. King, or no king."

"I'm just following orders miss."

"Who's orders?"

"The kings."

Calia seethed, and stood up tall to the guard, despite appearing two thirds his height. "Now listen... I don't know who you are, or when you became a guard, but you're going to learn one thing very quickly..." The guard moved back and adjusted his stance.

"Off you go." He said, gesturing to the alley behind him that led inside the castle.

Calia stopped, confused. She composed herself and pushed past him. Calia was often known for her fierce stubbornness, and despite her diminutive size, few were happy to be on the receiving end of a scolding from her. Even so, she felt a little perturbed that she was not given the full opportunity to offload onto the guard. She was full of anger and disappointment, and had just found a worthy place to unload it. To be cut off before she'd even had a chance to get going had left her even more angry and frustrated. As she shoved his shield when pushing past him, he gave one last glib remark, but she did not hear; she was too angry and just wanted to get home.

"The speeches have finished. You're free to go."

28

THE LAST DINNER

Jori enjoyed the warm embrace of his sons. They had gathered round him to congratulate him on his successful speech and hugged him lovingly.

"Are you sure it went well?" He said anxiously.

"Of course it did, father." Said Edevus proudly.

"I just would have expected more."

"More? They love you, it's plain to see. I've never heard such loud and generous applause."

"Yes, I suppose you are right. I was just expecting more questions, more reaction." Edevus turned his gaze to Necerta, who stared back at him nonplussed.

"Yes, they were a bit quiet." He said, his eyes still firmly on her.

"Maybe they were a bit shocked father, it's understandable in their position. I'm sure their questions will come in time." said Grimmd, placing a hand on his father's shoulder.

"Yes, yes… as wise as always. I just would have hoped to answer them myself. To feel like they really appreciated the scale of my gesture. To involve the people in the running of a kingdom, it's unheard of… it's…"

"…Very generous father." Interrupted Edevus. "I'm sure they were not being ungrateful. I'm sure that they will come to understand in time. Like you say, it is a very unusual and significant gesture."

"And quite unexpected too." Added Grimmd. "Do not dwell on it, father. You have been building up to this day for weeks now, and now that it's finally over you are bound to feel a bit empty. And you are likely very tired. May I suggest some rest?"

"No, no rest for me yet, I am to vacate this castle, say my farewells and set up lodging in the city." His face fell at the thought of it. What he had previously seen as an exciting new adventure now began to feel like exile; cast out of the castle by his own hand. He had thought a great deal about leaving the castle, but now that the time had come, he did not feel ready.

"Are you sure that's the right thing to do, father? So soon?" said Grimmd softly.

"Yes, no point dragging it out and delaying the inevitable."

"Yes, we wouldn't want to stand in your way and prevent you from starting your next adventure… but what about one night? We could all share one last meal together in the hall, invite some friends, perhaps? There is a lot to celebrate after all."

"I suppose there is. One last night in the hall? That does sound tempting."

"Oh yes father, we shall make it the grandest night of all. One final night."

"I don't know about grand, and I'm not sure who I would invite. I haven't heard a word from my generals in weeks... not what you expect from 'friends'. No, I would like to have a meal, but family only; you six and my dear staff."

"Of course, father. We will begin the plans immediately. But now father, please get some rest; we want you in fine form this evening." He beamed a generous smile towards Jori, who returned the gesture. *One last night in the hall* he thought.

The new kings and their queens were already seated by the time Calia and the cooks had arrived. Suddenly they felt understaffed. Four personal staff for one king was almost too much, but spread among six newer, younger rulers would surely stretch them too far. Calia and the old ladies had washed and had put on their best clothes. Although there wasn't much call for fancy clothes in their day to day lives, Jori had always ensured that they were never short of the nicer things that life had to offer. Calia wore a dark blue dress that flowed down to her toes. Mrs. Buxhall wore a loose fitting but elegant black dress and Mrs. Haughley wore a slightly tight-fitting red dress, a decision she clearly regretted, judging by her matching red face.

"Don't you all look splendid?" Said Stulta earnestly.

"Thank you, Your Majesty." Said Mrs. Buxhall, blushing.

"Where is Viga?" Asked Avarico abruptly.

"He will be fetching the king your highness."

"The king?" responded Avarico with his eyebrows raised.

"Sorry, Your Majesty, I mean no offence. It's just going to take some getting used to is all."

"Do not worry about it. Like my father said, we are all family now, you are safe here with us." Avarico's warmth was unexpected. The staff could not recall more than ten times that he had spoken to them since his arrival, but here he was, sipping wine, smiling kindly at them.

"Would you like some wine?" Offered Necerta.

"Yes please, just a small glass." Said Calia, hiding her eagerness to take the edge off their awkward situation. The older ladies were not so tactful, holding their glasses outstretched with visible excitement.

"Ahh, Viga dear boy… you made it. And where is our father?"

"He's on his way. I've dressed him, but he needs another short rest before he can come and join us. He really is very tired. He said not to wait for him, and that we should eat."

"Not to worry my lad, come and sit. Have some wine." Offered Edevus, gesturing theatrically to the table.

There they sat, they laughed and they drank. By the time the food had arrived, the whole table was in high spirits.

"I must say, it feels quite extraordinary to eat a meal that we haven't cooked." Said Mrs. Buxhall, her eyes slightly glazed and her cheeks red.

"We wouldn't dream of having you cook your own meal on a special night such as this. We have asked a company outside the castle to cater for us tonight. Our treat."

"Well, it's very much appreciated." She responded, raising her glass.

"I hope this isn't going to be the start of a new way of doing things." Said the usually quiet Mrs. Haughley.

"How do you mean, dear?" asked Grimmd.

175

"Food from outside the castle. If we did this every day we would be out of a job."

"Of course not, this is only a special occasion, where you are invited. I promise that all other culinary exercises will be carried out solely by the two of you, although I fear you may need some extra hands in the kitchen."

"You are probably correct, Your Majesty. Would we be permitted such an expense?" said Mrs. Buxhall, raising an eyebrow in the direction of Grimmd.

"Of course, dear. Like I said, we are family. Our arrival here is not to make your lives more difficult. Our father may have decreed for you to stay, but we hope that you would do so happily."

"Oh, well that's very kind of you, Your Highness. Very kind of you all." Beamed Mrs. Buxhall.

"Very Kind." Echoed Mrs Haughley. The kings turned their attention to Calia and Viga.

"Oh yes your highnesses. Very kind indeed. And will you be needing extra staff for your quarters?" said Calia gratefully.

"Yes, I imagine so. Would you be able to organise that? We would hate for you to have to manage staff that you weren't comfortable with." Said Grimmd.

"Manage?" said Calia quizzically, with a hint of excitement.

"Yes, a young and capable girl like yourself should be rewarded for your efforts. We would like you to oversee the staff in the residential suites, as these lovely ladies do in the kitchens… Less of the unpleasant work."

"Oh, well, that would be very nice. Thank you." Calia was beginning to feel quite foolish for mistrusting the men so far. They had done nothing to deserve her scepticism, and now that she thought about it, had showed her nothing but kindness. Their eyes now turned in the direction of Viga, but they were not met with a response. It was clear that the previous conversations had gone unnoticed to him, as he sat numbly staring at the flames of the large open fire that heated the room. No one was sure when Viga had become so inebriated, but the three women who knew him were not surprised.

"Oh Viga, for goodness' sake. How much wine have you had?" asked a clearly frustrated Calia.

"How much wine have *you* had?" he responded wittily.

"Two glasses. Your turn."

"*Two glasses.*" He responded with a crooked smile, clearly pleased with his retort.

"Your kings are addressing you, brother. Would you care to concentrate?"

"*Your* kings are addressing you..." he said smugly. "...Oh. Oh shit!" The reality of the situation had struck him at last. Viga was made to feel at ease, and the wine had made him if anything... too comfortable, but he was still in the presence of his kings and queens. It was common for Jori to see Viga in this state; if he ever attended the evenings in the grand hall with his king, or if he came home late after a night in the city with his friends. Each time, Calia would pick up his duties, helping the equally intoxicated king into his bed.

Attempting to appear soberer, he straightened his back and raised his eyebrows. "Sorry your highness... ssess... highnessessess." He drew a deep breath. "...I am sorry... I was caught in thought and did not notice that you were addressing me. Please proceed." The three men grinned. Edevus raised a glass to the young man.

177

"Not to worry young lad… we've all been there." Viga was relieved. He looked cautiously towards Calia, who was scorning him with her stare, he looked back at the kings.

"As we were saying to your sister, the kings command to have you work within the castle does not mean that you have to do so in your current role." Said Grimmd. "We would like you to take on a more senior position within the castle."

Viga looked cautiously towards his sister. "Promotion." She said under her breath.

"Oh! Yes, thank you your… thank you my Kings."

"We would like you to take on the security of the castle. To become our new…" Edevus paused for dramatic effect. "…Captain of the Castle Guards."

"*Captain.*" Viga whispered, his eyes glazed from the prospect of his new title… along with the wine. Calia smiled at him and punched him gently on the arm.

"You were right!" she said proudly.

As the evening drew on, Calia and the cooks got to know their new masters well, and the better they knew them, the more foolish Calia felt. Edevus had clearly inherited his father's love of attention, holding court as Jori had, only a few months ago, with long drawn out stories of their adventures in the North-East.

Grimmd was as witty as his predecessor, having the entire table laughing uproariously at several points in the evening. Avarico was a good sport, and extremely knowledgeable; his insight and comprehension of a wide variety of subjects captivated their guests throughout the evening.

Necerta shared her husband's wit and humour, combining to create a formidable double-act. She was interested in the lives and stories of all four staff members and her genuine attentiveness and curiosity made them feel both welcome and appreciated. While Stulta may have stumbled through some of Avarico's more complex musings, she was kind and complimentary to all throughout the evening. Frigus was not suited to dinner parties, nor any other kind of protracted social engagement. Whilst she had remained quiet for a considerable portion of the evening, the input she did have was well considered and thought provoking, she clearly shared an affinity with her husband for the more intellectual side of life.

By the time dessert had come, Calia, who had been softened considerably by more wine, had realised that they were still a man short. She felt terrible. "Oh no, we've been down here and Jori is missing out on all the fun."

"Oh yes, our dear father, I do hope that he's not too tired." Said Grimmd.

"Why don't you go and check on him Viga, your last act as a lowly man servant." Viga did not like to be referred to as a servant, but let this insult pass as he was enjoying himself too much, and did not want to spoil the mood. From this day on, it would not be an issue that he would have to deal with. This brought him great comfort and pride.

"That's captain Viga to you!" He slurred jovially. The room erupted in laughter.

"Of course, our noble captain… If you would be so kind to assist in your former duties." Chuckled Avarico, who seemed to find the wine as agreeable as any around the table.

"If it is not beneath a man of your high standing." laughed Edevus.

Calia looked on happily. The kind of response that Viga had just delivered to his kings would not have gone unnoticed by Jori in his rule, and certainly would not have been enjoyed in the spirit that the new kings had taken it. Maybe this was the change the Jori was talking about, new kings, new rules and a new way of doing things. *I could get used to this*, she thought as she sat back comfortably in her chair to listen to Edevus recount another tale.

29

THE NEWS

By the time Viga had returned to the hall, music was being played. Edevus was leading the group in an old song that he had recently learned from his father, their faces glowing happily in the candlelight. It took some time for them to feel Viga's presence, but when they did, the music stopped and the room fell cold and silent. Viga did not need to say the words that they all dreaded, they were written plainly on his pale, distraught face. "It's Jori. He's dead."

"Dead?" asked Avarico, looking stunned.

"Yes. He must have passed in his sleep."

"Let us check, this can't be so." Said Edevus, his voice cracking.

"I'm quite certain Your Majesty. He's cold and still... and..."

"It's OK Viga, we will take it from here. Are you OK?" Calia put her arm around her pale brother and sat him down.

She looked up at the three brothers, who were all sharing concerned looks with each other.

"We should all go. He may be our father, but you were also his family." Said Grimmd. Viga stayed behind as the rest headed up the long staircase, his shaking hands struggling to clasp the glass of wine that Calia had given him to steady his nerves, his eyes finally filling with tears.

"I can't believe this. It isn't right." Said Edevus.

"He was supposed to be starting his new journey, his peaceful days." Said Necerta, putting her hand gently on the shoulder of Grimmd.

"What were we all thinking?" Grimmd said solemnly.

"How do you mean?" asked Stulta.

"Down there, all of us. Singing and drinking while our father and king lay up here… alone."

"We weren't to know, dear." Soothed Mrs. Buxhall.

"He didn't come down. Not one of us went to check him. We could have helped." Replied Grimmd.

"What could we have done? His passing was inevitable. Too soon, I agree, but there's not a lot we could do. The day had obviously taken its toll."

"We could have been there for him. So that he wouldn't die alone. Someone, to hold his hand, someone to tell him it's OK." Grimmd cast his eyes at Calia, who had been standing further back, silent. She felt that she was being called on for her thoughts, but she had none to give. She felt the weight of Grimmd's words as they hung heavy over her. She may not be his daughter, but she should have been the one by his side, it's what she had planned. She would visit his house in the town every day to see how he was, and to let him know that despite his solitary new life, he would never be alone, not when he had her. She had failed him when he needed her the most. Mrs. Haughley saw the look in Calia's eyes and interjected.

"We should *all* have been here, or at least, he should have been with us." she said.

"Yes. We should. It shall be a burden that we will have to carry." Added Avarico, touching Calia gently on the arm. This was the first of any kind of physical contact or warmth that she had experienced from him, and it was welcome.

"Times like this are when we all have to work together." Said Edevus, as he stood firmly by his father's side. "We will have to deal with this matter in the proper way and make arrangements for his funeral. Mrs. Buxhall, could you send for the doctor so that he can do all the necessary checks and procedures?"

"Checks and procedures? The man is centuries old, I'm not sure what he would check for." Said the old lady.

"Yes, that is true, but we must follow the same protocol that we would for anyone."

"But Your Majesty, that's not what we usually do for anyone, and we haven't had a king die before."

"Well it's what we do now, OK?"

"As you wish Your Majesty."

Calia and the cooks set about clearing the dining hall of the aftermath of their callous celebrations. Every empty bottle and dirty plate a bitter reminder of their disregard for the man they claimed to admire so much. The three ladies said nothing to each other, but Mrs. Haughley would make efforts to exchange comforting glances with Calia. She was old and she knew the young girl well; she knew how this could affect her if she did not intervene. After several missed opportunities, she managed to approach Calia. As she sidled up to her, Calia could sense the platitudes that were making their way towards her.

"My dear girl, you shouldn't blame yourself for any of this. He was an old man, older than any other." Said Mrs. Haughley.

"Yes Mrs. Haughley. It may surprise you, but I did not think that I could somehow stop our King from passing. I'm not able to cheat death."

"Easy now girl, we're all very emotional, but let's not be too snarky."

"Snarky? Well how should we be? Happily dancing and singing while a scared old man dies alone?"

"All I was saying my dear is that you shouldn't take this on yourself. You're not to blame."

"Then who is?"

"No-one dear. That's what I'm trying to say."

"But we weren't there for him. We should have been there. *I* should have been there."

"But you weren't to know, where you? How could you?"

"Because he didn't come down. I was too busy having fun to notice that he hadn't come down. I should have checked on him."

"Like Viga said, he told us to carry on without him. We were letting him rest."

"You can tell yourself that if you like."

"Now listen here." Burst Mrs. Buxhall. "It's a terrible thing that's happened today. A terrible thing indeed. But there's nothing to be gained from blaming each other, or blaming ourselves."

"He was alone. He needed me and I wasn't there. You may be able to wipe your consciences clean, but I cannot."

Calia threw down her broom and stormed out of the room. She threw an angry look at Viga, instructing him to accompany her, but he remained seated and stared blankly at the large empty room; she huffed loudly at him and slammed the door behind her. Viga had remained in his chair since the others had gone to see the deceased king. His wine had slipped in his hand, his shoulders slumped forward. The guilt that was tormenting Calia had taken hold of Viga, leaving him empty and helpless.

Once the ladies had finished cleaning the hall around him, they turned their attentions to the young man. Mrs. Buxhall stood beside him and leaned over, holding his hands in hers. "It's OK my boy. There's nothing you could do. I know it's hard, but you did everything you could. You looked after him and kept him company. He loved you, and he knew that you loved him." Viga looked up at her, his childlike eyes red and watery. "Now, what do you say we get some rest? I shouldn't think you would want to be alone, why don't you join us in our quarters tonight?

"OK." Said Viga, allowing the two stout ladies to help him out of his chair.

The following morning, Calia was woken by Mrs. Buxhall, who was flustered and unkempt. "We have a meeting downstairs Calia, we all have to be there! Hurry now, we're already late!" and with that, she scampered away to her own quarters to prepare herself, leaving Calia's door open. Calia was confused and lacked the urgency of Mrs. Buxhall. She slowly gathered herself, closed her door and got washed and dressed.

By the time she arrived downstairs in the hall, it was clear that the rest of them had been waiting for some time.

Meetings of this nature never usually took place and certainly not in this manner, but today was the first day of the new reign, and things were bound to be different. There was also the dreadful matter of Jori's passing that needed to be dealt with, although she did not know what she could do to assist with that.

The room was much fuller than she expected. The three brothers, standing proud as usual in front of their respective wives. The two old cooks stood either side of a tired and bedraggled Viga, like small, soft joists holding him upright. She looked at him quizzically for some reassurance, but he could hardly meet her gaze; it was clear that he had barely slept since she saw him the previous evening. Guilt suffocated her once more, *poor Viga... I should have been there for him,* she thought. Beside the three Kings were two rows of four guards, one on either side. It was unusual to see guards inside the dining hall, other than when they were not on duty and enjoying Jori's company and ale. In front of the wall of kings, queens and guards, stood Doctor Flempton.

Doctor Flempton was the head of all medical practice within the kingdom. When the kings had suggested getting a doctor to assess the deceased king, she did not expect them to call on the services of Doctor Flempton, but it seemed fitting, considering the patient.

"Thank you all for joining us, especially so early... But this matter could not be postponed." Said Edevus. Confused looks darted around the room. "I shall get straight to it." He continued "...As you know, the new protocol in this situation is seek a medical opinion, so that we can ascertain and record the cause of death. For records and official purposes."

"Ass... What? Your majesty?" asked Mrs. Buxhall meekly, clearly intimidated by the nature of the meeting.

186

"To find out how he died, and to write it down. For historical purposes."

"How he died? Well… isn't it…" Calia coughed loudly and glared at her.

"Let him finish." She said.

"And it's a good job that we did." Said Grimmd, the faintest hint of a smirk creeping into the corners of his mouth.

"Yes. We have brought Doctor Flempton in to assess the cause of death, as there is no better doctor in the kingdom. And it is his opinion that the cause of Jori's death, was… poison." The three ladies gasped and began to protest, Viga stood open mouthed, as he had remained since the night before.

"I will let Doctor Flempton explain his findings. This is a great surprise to us all. One that no one could predict or explain."

"Well, I will do my best to try to explain it, Your Majesty." Said Doctor Flempton. He was a wiry old man with a neat beard that only covered his jaw. He wore small square glasses and a long pale blue jacket. He held a stack of papers in his right hand and a cane in the other. "…I was called upon late last night to assess the incident with King Jori." Edevus scolded the doctor with his eyes and he continued undeterred. "…While examining him, I noticed darkening around Jori's abdomen, on closer inspection I discovered that the exact cause of death was severe liver failure." He looked around the room at the solemn monarchs and the four confused staff members. "…What I mean to say is that although Jori was very old, his passing was in fact due to something that he had ingested." The four faces were as puzzled as before, he continued. "It didn't take long to find the source of the poisoning, it was left right beside his bed. In the glass of water

187

left on his bedside table… I found traces of White Snakeroot." The four staff remained unwavering in their obvious confusion. "It is a poison. His water was poisoned." Gasps and protestations filled the room once more.

"No, he can't have been." Objected Calia. "Who would do that?"

"There is only one person who could have I'm afraid." Said Grimmd, as the Kings turned to face her brother. At that moment, the guards lurched forward and seized Viga, who remained open mouthed and limp.

30

EXONERATION

It had been two days and Calia was finally losing her grip on her emotions. There had been no visitors, only food delivered by guards three times a day. For all her questioning, her pleading and her shouting, they gave her no information... only that she was to stay in her room until her involvement in Jori's murder could be ruled out.

On the afternoon of the second day, tired from her relentless pounding on the door, she slumped down on her knees and gave up. Two days of torment, of torture. Her mind flicked between deep concern for Viga and doubting his innocence...which lead to guilt, that turned into anger. However angry she became, she could find no suitable place to direct it. Was it the Kings? Had they lied? Had the doctor fed them misinformation? Had Viga assisted the Kings passing? Did Jori poison himself? Of all these scenarios, none would bring her peace; from this moment onward, this feeling would be alien to her. All she could do was worry. She worried for Viga mostly, but she made time to worry for her horse Astrus, who had not seen her in days and would be lonely. Was anyone looking after him?

On the second evening, a knock came on her door. *Urgh, food*, she thought. The very idea of it making her feel sick. Despite the regular delivery of meals, clearly prepared by the hands of her friends, she could not stomach the thought of eating it. "Can I come in dear?" The soft, undulating tones of Mrs. Buxhall were beyond a relief to Calia. She opened the door and greeted the plump old lady with an embrace, almost squeezing the tray out of her hand. "Now, now, dear. Don't get too excited, I can't stay long. I've been instructed to make sure you eat your food. You've been returning full plates. And it won't do."

"Bollocks to the food, Mrs. Buxhall." said Calia abruptly. "...I'm sorry, I did not mean it like that. I'm just not hungry. How is Viga? That's what's important. Where is he? What is happening to him?"

"Just eat my dear, we can talk about that afterwards."

"Afterwards? No. You will tell me now. I won't eat until you do." Mrs. Buxhall raised her eyebrows and sat down on the bed beside Calia.

"The truth is, dear... that I don't know anything. None of us do. The castle is in full lock-down and there are guards everywhere."

"Where is Viga?"

"He's being held somewhere, I don't know where. But he's being held there for questioning."

"Questioning? But he didn't do it. What more can he tell them?"

"I know dear, I... I don't know what to say. We're as confused as you are. Nothing like this has ever happened inside this castle."

"Confused? You don't think he did it do you?"

"No, dear... of course not. Not young master Viga. How would he even devise such a cunning plan?" Calia managed to summon a wry smile.

"Why am I here then? Why can't I go back to work? Why can't I see Viga?"

"They just said that it's for the safety of the castle, once they know what happened, and can make sure we are all safe from further harm... you will be free."

"But they can't keep me here, I've done nothing wrong."

"An attack on one of us is an attack on us all. That's what King Grimmd says."

"And you believe that?"

"Well, yes. It might be for your own good my dear. What if it was someone other than Viga? They could come for you next, or Viga... or me!"

"Come for you? What for? Your jam tart recipe?"

"Yes, alright. You know what I mean. They are just making sure that we're all safe."

"What do you mean *what if it was someone else*? You *do* believe he did it, don't you?"

"Now... don't get yourself all worked up. You know full well that I didn't mean it like that. I was just saying that it's better to be safe than sorry. And if someone else poisoned Jori, it's all the more reason to stay safe."

"I suppose you're right. I'm sure that he will be free soon. We all will. They just need to find the real killer."

"That's right. Now... I told you all I know, so eat your food. Otherwise I'll end up locked in *my* quarters as well."

191

The next morning, Calia was broken from her tired, trance-like worrying by one of the guards stationed by her door. "Your Kings, Grimmd and Edevus are here to see you… Get up." Calia sprung up as if woken suddenly from a deep sleep and attempted to compose herself.

"We are deeply sorry for the intrusion Calia, but we didn't want to keep you any longer than necessary." Said Grimmd, and he slithered onto her bed beside her. Edevus propped one leg up on her sideboard and addressed her more formally than she expected.

"Dear girl, this is a very unusual and unfortunate situation. It is with great sadness that the crown's investigation into the death of our father concluded that Viga *was* responsible for the poisoning of the former king."

"No, that's not true, it can't be." Calia looked around for reassurance, but only found sympathetic faces, solemnly nodding. Necerta and Stulta were accompanying their husbands, standing in the doorway attempting to look as comforting and compassionate as they could.

"We're so sorry Calia." Said Stulta, with the most genuine of all the caring faces.

"Although this news may be difficult for you to hear, there is some kind of silver lining at least." Said Edevus.

"Silver lining? My brother murdered The King!" Said Calia, tired and exasperated.

"Former King." Seethed Edevus. "However… none the less, it is an act of treason. As is any form of corroboration or assistance." The intention in his eyes was clear. Calia moved herself further up the bed, away from her new employers. She was suddenly aware of not only how bad things were for Viga, but how much trouble *she* could be in.

"I swear, I didn't know anything." She said, her voice much less sure than it was a second earlier.

"We know. We know that you would never hurt your former king, you loved him, and he loved you." The relief flooded into Calia's face and she exhaled wearily. She paused for a second and shared an obvious thought.

"…but so did Viga. Viga loved Jori, he wouldn't have done this."

"That's what we thought." Said Grimmd. "We would have never have thought him capable. But unfortunately, he confessed."

"Confessed?" Calia was upright in her bed and confused.

"Yes, under questioning by the royal guards. He confessed to poisoning the old man before he slept."

"But why?" Calia's voice was cracking.

"He said that he felt abandoned by the King. He was expecting promotion, but was instead instructed to stay in his current role for the rest of his days. He felt that he was betrayed. Little did he know…"

"… That you were going to grant him his wish at dinner anyway." Calia interrupted.

"Indeed. It seems that your brother was a victim of his own ambition. And so was our father." Said Grimmd. Calia stared into nothingness, her face devoid of all life or emotion. After the kings allowed her time to process the news, Grimmd moved closer and put his hand on hers. Edevus cleared his throat, drawing her attention back to him.

"As I was saying…" He steadied himself on his raised leg, his pre-planned announcement hanging excitedly over him. "…The good news in all of this, is that we have decided not to interrogate or prosecute you."

"Oh?" Said Calia, more confused than relieved.

"Yes, have decided that if you say that you had no knowledge of Viga's terrible plans, that we will take you on your word and you will face no further investigation." He looked down at her expectantly. It was an uncomfortable amount of time before Calia picked up on his obvious cue.

"Oh, no… of course not. I knew nothing of the sort."

"Good, and you will remain loyal to your new kings?"

"Of course. More now than ever."

"Then so be it. You are free. What's more, we have decided that you may keep your position within the castle. Not only because you have our trust, but because it was the dying wish of a man whom you cared for deeply. A man who has been taken away from us by your brother. We are sure that your devotion in this role will make up for the anguish inflicted upon our father, by your brother."

"Yes, Your Majesty. Thank you. Sincerely, I thank you. You have my gratitude and devoted service, I swear."

"Good." Said Edevus, his pride swelling with the acceptance of her words. Grimmd held her hand tightly and smiled at her. His compassionate smile was a welcome comfort to her tired, disconsolate state. A glimmer of hope in such a dire situation.

31

THE GIFT HORSE

"How could he do this?" Calia paced angrily up and down the kitchen. The two old ladies sipped tea and shared sympathetic looks.

"I know dear." Said Mrs. Buxhall softly.

"How could he betray me like this?"

"Yes dear." Said Mrs. Haughley. Calia had been recycling the same conversation for over an hour now, and whilst the cooks sympathised deeply with Calia's plight, they had come to realise the futility of their involvement in the conversation. They had resigned themselves to sharing simple platitudes for some time now, and clearly Calia required more.

"Why would he do it? Not to Jori, but to us? Why would he do that to me?"

"I don't suppose that he did really my dear." Said the tired Mrs. Buxhall, who was beginning to miss the days when the young lady was confined to her quarters.

"He did, and it was selfish. He must have known that this would affect us like this."

"You know Viga, dear. He wasn't one for thinking things through." Mrs. Buxhall winced at the words as they left her mouth. Calia didn't notice, her anger far outweighing her sadness by this point.

"No, I don't suppose he did. But I still can't work out why. He can't have expected to get promoted once Jori left, that was just a joke between the two of us. He can't have taken it *that* seriously."

"That's the part that hurts me the most. After all that, the boys gave Viga what he wanted anyway. It's just such a waste." Said Mrs. Haughley.

"A waste indeed. He was a good boy. It was a waste of two of our most treasured lives." Added Mrs. Buxhall. She raised her cup of tea into the air.

Calia leaned back on the kitchen counter.

"What's going to happen to us now?" She said. Her eyes had become more pensive, the fiery anger dampened. She almost looked scared.

"Oh, not much dear. Life will go on as usual. We will remember Jori, and it will get easier over time." Mrs. Buxhall seemed pleased with her words.

"No, not all that. What will happen to us, *here*? There were four of us, working for one good man, now we are three, working for... *them*."

"Now hold your tongue there, girl. Those three are good men and they have been good to us... you especially." Mrs.

Buxhall rose to her feet, although it did not alter her height a great deal.

"Me especially?" Asked Calia sharply.

"Yes. Of course. Firstly, your former King, of whom you were so fond... he left you with nothing. Destined to be a chamber made for all eternity. Those boys came in and without any reason to or any obligation... they gave you a promotion... you and Viga." Mrs. Buxhall had adopted her preaching stance. One hand was on her hip, the other holding an object to gesticulate with, in this case a rolling pin. Calia knew this stance all too well and took a seat. Whatever Mrs. Buxhall had to say, she was going to get it out, and there was nothing Calia could do to stop her.

"I know" Calia said, resignation creeping into her voice.

"On top of all of that, when your brother did what he did, did what no man has done before...what did they do? They kept it quiet. Have you even seen the news?"

"News?" Calia said confused.

"Yes, those printing presses that Jori used to use to get out papers to the kingdom. Well, now the boys have started using them to keep the people informed of what's going on in the castle."

"In the castle? Inside the castle?"

"Yes. Well, not about us or anything, just governance."

"*Governance*?" Calia raised a suspicious eyebrow towards Mrs. Buxhall.

"She learnt it in the newspaper. It's her new word." Said Mrs. Haughley, grinning.

"It means what they will be doing and how they will be doing it... with regard to ruling the kingdom." Mrs. Buxhall said proudly. Calia's eyebrow remained raised. "...and I for one think that it's a very good thing. It keeps the people informed. And they feel involved."

"But you *are* involved Mrs. Buxhall. You literally live here."

"Yes, but I don't rule the kingdom, do I?"

"No... at least we can be thankful for that." Said Calia, her eyebrow finally dropped and a smirk began to form at the corners of her mouth. "But what does this have to do with Viga?"

"Well, when you were in your bedroom, the kings issued a statement about the death of the former king, Jori."

"A statement? What did it say?"

"That he died of old age, peacefully in his sleep. He was old and there was nothing anyone could do."

"So... they lied?"

"You're missing the point dear. They could have brought public shame to you and your family, by pointing the finger at Viga, but they spared you that."

"My family? It's only me and Viga."

"Still, they could have told the world what your brother did, but they didn't. They did that to protect *you.*"

"Why would they do that?"

"The same reason they promoted you. The same reason they kept you on, even after what your brother did."

"And what is that?"

"Well, they love you. They see you as family." Mrs. Buxhall had finished waving her rolling pin in the air, and finally put it on the counter. Her point was made.

"And it's what Jori would have wanted. You can say what you like, but those boys have a great love and respect for their father." Mrs. Haughley said, glancing at her friend for approval as she did so.

"I hadn't really thought about it that way." Said Calia pensively.

"It's been a tough few days, girl… the toughest." Said Mrs. Buxhall "But just take note, and remember the good that people do for you… don't be so cynical."

Calia rinsed her wine glass and put it on the side, before making her way to the stables.

It had been four days since she had last seen Astrus. The kings had arranged for him to be fed and let out during her absence, but it was clear that he had missed her company. Astrus had been a sounding board for Calia since she was young.

A present from Jori, Astrus was deemed unfit for service due to his odd proportions. His legs were too long, and his head was too big. For a horse to be raised in the military, this would not be acceptable, and could cause all number of issues. Once Jori saw the deformed fowl, he knew the one person best suited for loving him. Jori knew of Calia's love of animals well. Ever since she had entered the castle as a young girl, she had been preoccupied with helping the animals around the castle. From saving tired bees in summer, to sheltering wild dogs in the winter, her heart was always full of love for the animals around her… none more so than Astrus.

Unbeknown to Jori and the military that served him, Astrus' unnatural dimensions and deformed features were a sign of what was to come. As Astrus grew, his physique eventually evened out and he turned out to be one of the most beautiful horses that you could imagine… the only issue was his size. Once fully grown, Astrus was the size of three horses combined. His powerful muscles covering his giant frame, Astrus was a sight to behold; a frightening and deeply intimidating beast. Despite his awkward size and undeniable strength, Astrus was as gentle as his owner. The love that

Calia had shown him since he was cast out was repaid to her with a gentle and unwavering loyalty.

When the military were made aware of what had become of the deformed fowl that they had abandoned, they immediately wanted him to return to their ranks. Despite never facing war, and having very little to fight in their long and uneventful history, the kingdoms army knew that their job would be a lot easier with a horse of that scale and power within their ranks. Fortunately for both Astrus and Calia, King Jori knew all too well of the love that they shared for each other; separating the two of them would result only in an assistant and horse who were both too unhappy to do their jobs properly. Despite his ultimate rule, Jori managed to appease the commanders with stories of how the horse may be enormous, but is unfit for fighting, having been raised with too much love, and not enough discipline; both of which were true statements.

That night, Calia took comfort in the company of her closest remaining friend, leaning on his side, musing for hours over her own misfortune, her brother's betrayal and the guilt she was beginning to feel for her lack of gratitude towards her new employers. Astrus was the perfect advisor, always listening and unlike the cooks or her disgraced brother, never offering an opinion.

32

AVENUES AND ALLEYWAYS

Jori was a father to the nation in the most absolute way, he commanded respect and reflected it back onto his subjects. The arrival and sudden appointment of his three sons brought with it a new relationship between the monarchy and those they ruled over. The natural charisma of Edevus, the pleasing words of Grimmd and the imposing power of Avarico inspired adoration from the population on a level that Jori could never have imagined.

The way the people of Jorisham idolised and revered their new rulers would have made Jori uncomfortable, but was welcomed and encouraged by his heirs. The way he had felt, standing above his subjects as they applauded and shouted in their support of him was unmatched by anything he had experienced in his short time as a man. The public address he had made at Jori's abdication had filled him with such a deep sense of purpose and power, that he had been searching to replicate it ever since.

It took only two days since the abdication for his newfound search for adoration to lead him to Lowston. It was Edevus' first visit in the noisy, messy avenues of Lowston, yet he felt more at home than he had since his arrival at the castle. He wandered through the streets, past cafes, bars and brothels, soaking in the chaos and the faintest sense of that feeling. It may have been subtle, almost imperceptible, but it was there... the feeling he got for the first time at Jori's abdication. Edevus drifted aimlessly through the alleyways, pulled by the feeling he craved the most. As he moved through, he could sense the feeling ebbing and flowing through him, growing stronger when he passed some people, only to flutter away again when passing others. He saw buskers, poets and authors, displaying their art to passers-by, occasionally striking a chord with their tiny audiences and releasing some of that feeling for him to absorb. Pulled in by a sense of that sensation, he walked through sparsely populated galleries with finely crafted artwork, and while he could see their beauty, it gave him no joy and that feeling escaped him once again.

As the day moved on, he began to grow frustrated. He stopped in a small cafe for some respite. The feeling existed, but so faintly that it was beginning to feel like torture. He had felt it in fleeting moments shared between performer and audience, emanating gently out from art galleries. Each time the feeling was there, it escaped him. The adoration that he had received on that balcony was his first and last taste, but it could not be replicated often. He needed to find a more reliable source. The art of Lowston was unmatched, but the audiences were small and distracted. People moved about the district with aimless purpose, all on their own quest for fulfilment, some instant and some more meaningful.

Edevus began to feel small. The mighty King, newly crowned, with the world at his feet, now reduced to yet another desperate lost soul in search of gratification. He would not have it... He would find the source of his contentment, no matter how long it took. With renewed vigour, he rose from his seat and set about on his quest.

"Hey! Aren't you going to pay for that?" a voice called after him sharply. He looked back to see a young lady behind the counter, who had brought him tea a few minutes earlier. Throughout his short life as a man, Edevus had been inside a carriage and a castle. Whilst the witches magic had gifted him with the knowledge of the world that he needed, courtesy of the late Mrs. Felsam... he had no true memories of his own. His gift as a story teller came not from his experience but his imagination, the positive reception that always accompanied his anecdotes was also in part due to interference from his wife. Edevus knew how the world worked, so he knew how cafes worked... but it was not instinctual for him.

"I'm sorry. My mind was elsewhere."

"That's OK. So...?" Her dark brown eyes bore into him with expectation and a little amusement. She was a tall, slender woman, similar in frame and height to the king himself. She had dark skin and a long face, her features and accent told the story of a woman from a more distant land. Edevus was intrigued by her, as she stood with her hands on her hips, one eyebrow raised and her long flowing black hair tied up with a strip of red fabric.

Despite entering, sitting and drinking a cup of tea, Edevus had not actually registered his surroundings. The cafe was small and dark, with light beaming in through the windows in sharp rays. The smell of tea, pipe smoke and exotic food filled his senses and he remained entranced by the waitress.

"Have you lost the ability to speak, as well as pay?" she continued. Edevus composed himself.

"I'm very sorry, my mind was elsewhere."

"So you said. Three Beccles please."

"Yes… of course…" He stammered. "Although, I didn't actually bring any money with me."

"How convenient. And what were you planning to pay for the tea with… a song?" the amusement grew in her eyes, Edevus felt small again.

"I can pay. I just don't have anything with me. I can get it from the castle."

"The castle?" she beamed. "What have we done down here to deserve a visit from a resident of the castle? What are you? A guard? You're too tall and handsome to be a servant!" Edevus almost blushed.

"I… am your king." He proclaimed loudly. The room fell silent. The eyes of the other customers rose up to him anxiously. Far from the ornamental gowns that he had worn to address his new subjects, his current attire was modest and understated; a mistake he would not make again. As nervous whispers shifted around the cafe, Edevus knew that he needed to fill the unbearable silence. "I have come here today to get to know my city more. To understand my people." He was looking directly at the unfamiliar looking cafe owner, but he was speaking as if he was projecting to hundreds. The woman stared back at him, her eyebrows had lowered, but the smile remained on her elegant, long face.

"So… you think that means you don't pay for tea do you?" the whispers floating around the cafe turned to murmurs, and the tension in the room grew thick. Edevus recoiled slightly with surprise.

"I would expect that you would take my word that I will pay in due course."

"I don't doubt that."

"Do you doubt that I am your king?"

"No, I am sure you are. I remember your face now, too handsome to forget." Edevus recoiled again. That was the second time that she had called him handsome, and she had not adjusted her tone or apologised after she found out who he was. Whilst he didn't know what reaction to expect from her, this certainly wasn't it. Her dark eyes stayed fixed on his, looking deeper into him than anyone had before.

"It's a pleasure Your Majesty." Said a voice from Edevus' right. He turned to see who had interrupted them and was met by a room full of blank, nervous faces. He knew that he should not make a scene, he was unguarded and in unfamiliar territory.

"The pleasure is all mine, good people." He replied to the room. He summoned the tone and sentiment of his brother Grimmd and continued. "I came here looking for ways to improve this part of the city, but instead I found ways that Lowston can improve the rest of Jorisham. This is a truly inspiration place, vibrant and expressive. 'The Jewel in the Crown of Jorisham' indeed." A warm applause followed, and the feint feeling returned. It felt good, but Edevus knew that this wasn't enough. It would never be enough. As the applause rippled gently through the dark room, he cast his gaze back to the enchanting waitress who now appeared busy with an order. She looked over and noticed his hopeful stare, then gestured for him to leave with a warm smile. Edevus' mind returned to the task at hand.

As he left the cafe, his head was muddled, but he knew what he was looking for. He pushed the thoughts of the waitress from his mind and focused. He knew that the adoration of the public for the simple act of being a king would grow old soon, he had to find another path. He wandered faster than before through the winding labyrinth of alleyways, further and further into Lowston.

The further he ventured, the darker it became. The clean, sandy stones that made up the majority of Jorisham seemed like a distant memory, replaced by cold dark grey, damp stone and slate. The cafes and bars were now brothels and smoking dens, there were no buskers, no poets and no art. The feeling that had tormented him throughout his journey into the dark district had all but disappeared. He noticed the empty feeling that was beginning to take hold of him and decided to turn back.

At the point where he had made his decision to stop and retreat, he felt a flicker once more. It was faint as always, no more than an idea of the feeling, but it was different. He moved forward once again, this time faster. He was practically running through the streets when he finally found it.

At the end of a long, narrow alley... a tall, thin building. It wasn't much to look at, a simple grey structure with a tall, pointed roof. It wasn't the sight of the building that drew Edevus in, it was the sound. Low groans and wails came emanating from the odd building, flowing down the alley towards him... and with it, the feeling. This wasn't how he felt when he was being applauded, or when his stories were being appreciated, this was different. It was not for *him*.

He carefully opened the large heavy. In front of him was a modest hall with no more than thirty people, all kneeling on the floor in the direction of one man. Their eyes were shut as they groaned and moaned in unison at the command of the man in front.

"Do you feel it? Can you feel the energy flowing towards you?" his voice was soft and whispering, yet loud enough for all to hear. His arms were moving as if they were made of water. His bald head reflected the candlelight in the room, and his pale-yellow robes danced beneath him like smoke. He had found it. This is where he needed to be. This is who he needed to be. In his short time in the kingdom, Edevus had come to learn that he enjoyed being adored. Whilst he could achieve this as king, what he saw there in Lowston offered him the chance to be more than just adored, he could be worshipped.

Jori had maintained a strict separation between ideology and government. In truth, he had never fully understood Lowena's fascination with the deeper questions that life has to offer, although many among his care did. Strict rules were put in place over what could be said in public without being substantiated. While these rules had their practical uses, they were a selfish act on behalf of the former king. If Jori's subjects viewed another being as higher than himself, his rule would be a lot more difficult. The result of the regulations on public speech led to all spiritual gatherings having to be conducted under the lawless cover of Lowston's deeper recesses.

Having unearthed such an unusual spectacle, Edevus knew that he had to have a piece of it. As a king, and with all the powers that accompany the title, Edevus was able to create the Kingdom's first legal and open religion; 'The Church of Enlightenment'. The aims of the church were intentionally vague. With promises of hope and wellbeing, happiness and wealth, it was easy for the church to grow rapidly. The people of Jorisham were unaccustomed to such wild and mysterious claims and those who heard the claims, willingly followed with absolute certainty from the outset.

33

THE JORISHAM CHRONICLE

The Death of Jori

It is with great sadness that we report the death of the former King of Jorisham. Jori has been the king of Jorisham since its beginning. He founded, built and grew the kingdom from nothing. Today's news follows the formers Kings public abdication yesterday.

The cause of Jori's death was natural. Senior physician Doctor Flempton issued the following statement, 'As the longest living man on record, his death is not unexpected, but a shock nonetheless. Jori had seen his health suddenly decline in recent weeks. He passed peacefully in his sleep, with no signs of external influence. The only medical question here is not how Jori died, but how he had managed to live for as long as he did.'

The citizens of Jorisham are invited to a public wake at the castle before the annual harvest celebrations begin. Loyal subjects are asked to bring donations in Jori's name, which will be given to those in need.

The Church of Enlightenment meets in two days

For those lost souls still unaware of the Church's teachings, there will be an open ceremony held in two days' time at the great assembly hall. Our great new leader, father Edevus, will be leading the blessings, during which he will call for a fruitful and prosperous harvest. Father Edevus issued the following statement.

'As your leader, in both the pragmatic and spiritual senses, I can assure you of one thing... truth. To prove that the teachings are correct, and that our lord not only speaks to me, but listens to me... I am calling on to him to provide a harvest like none has ever seen. If this call is answered, even those who are currently ignorant of the lord's powers will be fools to ignore them.'

The Central Crop Trust Expands

The keeper of the coin, King Avarico, has successfully expanded the reach of the central agricultural trust. Under the rule of Jori, many farms within the trust had decided to work independently from the trust. Avarico and the trust wish these farmers well, and have managed to replace their memberships with those from further outside the kingdom walls.

This is not only good news for the trust, but good news for the kingdom, as more towns and villages become members of the trust, the kingdom will be able to generate more coin, which will be passed down to you, the people.

***

"Have you seen this?"

"What's that my dear?"

"These letters, they are spread all across the city." Calia had returned from her errands outside the castle walls with a fistful of papers. Her temper was raging again. Mrs. Buxhall sat her down and took the papers from her tight grip.

"Oh yes, dear… this is what we were telling you about. These are the newspapers that the kings have distributed to tell people about the old king's death."

"And you're OK with this?"

"OK with it my love? Of course. There's not a word about young master Viga on it, and not a word about what he's done, neither."

"Not that, the funeral."

"Yes, we know about the funeral, dear… what do you think we're so busy preparing for?"

"It's just before the harvest celebrations."

"Yes, I thought that was a nice thought."

"A nice thought?" Calia had risen from her seat and picked up the papers once more. "They are burying our king and then celebrating the harvest! As if it doesn't matter!"

"Well, what do you expect them to do? Cancel the harvest?"

"Of course! Yes! They *should* cancel it."

"And what purpose would that serve? More unrest? More unhappiness? More questions?"

"So, we are just brushing it under the carpet, are we?"

"I wouldn't think that was altogether a bad idea… especially for you, dear."

"I know what you're trying to say… and I don't like it."

"You never seem to, these days." Mrs. Haughley piped up from across the room. She was hunched over the sink, furiously peeling an extraordinary mound of potatoes.

"What do you mean by that?" said Calia, surprised at sharp tone used by the usually mild and considered old lady.

"Well, ever since this awful business has happened, you haven't liked to listen to anything we have to say. We understand how hurt you are, but you're not the only one who's upset. With all that's happened, we have been given a second chance here. To live in the past and keep getting all worked up will do none of us any good."

Calia said nothing. Mrs. Buxhall raised her eyebrows theatrically at her and smugly sipped her tea; a prop that she had seemingly conjured up for this exact moment. Mrs. Haughley's gaze remained fixed firmly on her peeling.

"I'm sorry." Said Calia eventually. "It's been a difficult time. I'm worried about Viga and what's to come… for all of us."

"Well, you needn't worry about us." Said Mrs. Buxhall. "The Kings are kind and fair… and they are treating us well. This is the best we can expect from such an awful situation. The best by a long shot."

"You are right, I'm sorry."

"Of course we're right, girl. Now stop apologising and go and help Mrs. Haughley with those potatoes, before does herself a mischief."

34

MEMORIAL DAY

Colourful flags and banners adorned the walls and hung from the roofs surrounding the castle courtyard. The people beneath them already a sea of purple, yellow and green.

It seemed like only moments before, that the three new kings were standing on the balcony addressing their subjects. The three pillars of a new Jorisham; proud and tall, strong and confident. The three queens provided a supportive backdrop as always, with guards either side, framing the three men. Despite their reign lasting no more than one week, the three kings had made their presence felt throughout the kingdom. Unlike the understated and practical speeches made by Jori, his sons adopted a more theatrical approach when addressing their subjects.

Adorned in their respective colours; Edevus in purple, Grimmd in yellow and Avarico in green, the three men stood for some time, happily receiving the waves of admiration and reverence... none more so than Edevus.

With their subjects below them, and the rapturous applause finally subsiding... the kings made their solemn address. Edevus stood proud, absorbing the attention and adoration of those beneath him. He paused and smiled, then began.

"People of Jorisham, thank you for joining us on this very sad day. The saddest the kingdom has ever known. Jori may have been our father, but he was also, in many ways... yours. We share your grief, as you do ours. Summing up Jori's life with words has been the hardest task that we have faced to date. You all know of his accomplishments; the city you live in is evidence of those... but so are you. Each one of you good people are a living testament to the strength and compassion that our father built this kingdom on. For all of you standing here today, there has been no life before Jori; he and his kingdom existed long before any of us here. Sadly, only his kingdom remains. Our task now is to ensure that the kingdom of Jorisham not only continues to survive... but to thrive.

With this new age, we bring hope and opportunity to all. Life under Jori was hard and it was long. The kingdom we all know and love has been standing still for too long.

We stand on the precipice of a new era. An era of change, of progress and prosperity. We are here to guide you through this new dawn, out from the shadows of mediocrity and into the light."

Edevus opened his arms and welcomed the deafening noise that followed. He took a step backwards and let Grimmd come forward to speak. His manner was a stark contrast to the wide, authoritative stance of his brother. Grimmd lowered his shoulders and clasped his hands together apologetically.

"This is what we want for you, our people. But we cannot do this alone. We need your support. We need your trust. We need you to trust that our decisions are in your best interests, even if it may not seem that way. From where you are standing, what can you see? You can see us, you can see what we do, but you cannot see each other, not all of you. From up here we can see all of you, we can see the whole city. Most importantly, we can see beyond. From here, we can see the horizon, and that is why we need your trust. We need you to let us see for you, to let us make the right decisions for Jorisham, but most importantly... for you." The applause that followed pleased him greatly, although not as much as it did Edevus. As Grimmd took his steps backwards, it left only Avarico at the front of the balcony. A man of very few words, his powerful presence brought with it an air of apprehension.

"My brothers and fellow kings ask little of you, yet they give you so much." His harsh tone was expected, yet it subdued the crowd, nonetheless. "We ask only for loyalty, and in return grant your safety and prosperity. Our reign has been short, but already we have begun to forge a new path for this kingdom... a path to a better future. Only one week ago, the great Edevus called upon our lord to provide us with a fruitful and profitable harvest. As your keeper of coin, I can confirm the returns for the harvest for this year." He paused.

The harvest celebrations were always preceded with the announcement on returns, but never along with a funeral. Edevus began to step forward as his large brother continued.

"This year's harvest has brought in over five times more than any harvest on record." The applause that followed eclipsed any noise that the kingdom has experienced before.

Edevus stood at the front of the balcony, glowing with pride and self-satisfaction. He allowed the gratitude to flow over him for some time until it eventually died down.

"I hope that now, you can see the true power of our lord, and the faith that he has in your kings." The response was deafening. "…To reward the loyalty that you have shown us, and the faith that some of you have placed in our lord, we are extending the harvest celebrations to the entire kingdom. In honour and remembrance of our father. We invite you all to join us this evening within the castle walls, to celebrate the life or Jori and the unprecedented harvest this year.

By the time the last of the kings had left the grand balcony, the kingdom was a frenzied whirlwind of excitement. Only a select few were able to attend the grand harvest celebrations each year. Farmers from across the lands mixed with army generals and royal advisers, even a few foreign visitors. This year, every humble shopkeeper and factory worker would be able to see inside the castle walls and experience what they could have only previously imagined. The streets were full of people frantically rushing to prepare. Vendors were hastily assembling mobile stores, tailors and haberdasheries were packed to the rafters. Every man and woman feverishly preparing for the most exciting night they would likely ever experience.

By the time the evening came, the city was awash with colour. People flooded into the streets and made their way to the castle. The castle itself was vast. A huge empty vessel with imposing halls, each with enormous, ornate domed ceilings. The fact that only a few people could admire the beauty of the inside of the castle was a terrible waste.

Jori knew the importance of status. He had built the castle to be admired and to inspire. The aspiration of those beneath him was one of the most successful motivators that he had witnessed; access to his inner circle was only appealing if it brought with it rewards. The reward for those inside the castle was clear to see. Jori also knew that danger was never far. Cautious from his experience with the barbarian army generations before, Jori had built the castle as a garrison inside the city. Large enough to fit most of his subjects, not comfortably... but safely at least.

On the night of the harvest celebrations, most citizens were accommodated within the great halls, passageways and courtyards of the great castle. Those that were not, lined the surrounding streets of the castle, with people mixing in and out of the castle gates freely.

Food vendors began to appear outside as the festivities flowed merrily into the surrounding area. The castle was awash with noise, music and laughter. Rows of large candles lined each hall and courtyard, their flames dancing in unison with the overjoyed and overwhelmed guests. The large main hall remained reserved for the celebrations more 'traditional' guests. Generals, commanders and captains shared stories and wine with leaders of industry and commerce. The seats usually occupied by the head farmers were now filled with religious leaders and lawyers, sharing giant platters of food, prepared by the castle staff. The food was simple yet plentiful and the wine flowed freely.

At the head of the largest table, sat the three brothers. Their table was raised higher than any other, allowing them to look down on their new allies; and for them all to look up in return, in awe.

"And you think this will work Grimmd?" Said Avarico warily. "It's not just to pamper Edevus' vast ego?" Edevus looked across at his large, stiff brother with malice. Grimmd replied softly.

"Have more wine, dear brother. Enjoy this moment. Look out there and tell me what you see."

"Fools. Drinking and eating themselves silly on my coin." Said Avarico angrily.

"True. And what are fools, brother?"

"A waste of time and money."

"No. Fools are easily led. Fools, dear brother... are loyal."

35

FAMILY REUNION

"I need to see him." Said Calia. She frowned pensively through the window, holding a hot cup of tea in her tired, trembling hands. The two ladies that she was addressing sat slumped over the main table in the kitchen, exhausted and depleted.

"What's that, dear?" Said Mrs. Buxhall faintly, clearly hoping for a short response.

"Viga. I have to go and see him."

"What? Now? What's brought all this on?" Mrs. Buxhall sighed and straightened her back, clearly unprepared for this type of conversation.

"I feel like I've betrayed him."

"Betrayed who? Viga? Don't be silly girl, if anyone has done the betraying, it's your foolish brother."

"I haven't visited him."

"I don't think anyone has, dear… and for good reason."

"I haven't even been once though, I haven't seen him since they took him away."

"And what's changed?"

"I was angry with him, I was hurt."

"And has that changed so much?"

"No, I don't suppose so. But he's still my brother. I should see how he is. I'm worried."

"I'm sure they are taking good care of him down there. And that's the most he can ask for after all he's done. Can't this wait? Why are you bringing this up now?"

"I was just thinking of him. If he were here, we would be out there, dancing among the lights and music."

"Well don't let us stop you girl!" Mrs. Buxhall gave a broad smile and raised her bushy eyebrows in the direction of Mrs. Haughley, who was now fast asleep, face down on the table. "Now, if you don't mind… I must bring Mrs. Haughley back to life and take her to bed. This has been the longest and hardest day of work that I can remember."

"I hear that it will be like this every year." Said Calia, as she collected their cups to be washed.

"I can't imagine that could be true. It looks like this all cost quite a bit of money, I don't think they could keep it up every year."

"I don't think *you* could either."

"You're not wrong there, girl. Now off you go. Enjoy the night… Enjoy your youth." And with that, the old lady creaked up from her chair and shook her friend awake. Calia took off her apron and straightened her clothes.

"You are not authorised to be here."

The guard didn't even look down to address Calia. He was a tall man, his heavy armour only adding to his intimidating presence. He stood in front of a large wooden door, reinforced with steel. It was secured with a huge wooden bar that spanned the wide opening, plunging deep into the stone walls either side. At his side was a dense, complicated ring of keys.

"I am a resident of this castle, and I would like to visit a prisoner.

"Which prisoner?"

"Which one? How many are there?"

"Which... prisoner?"

"Viga." Calia hesitated. "I would like to see master Viga please."

"The traitor?" the guard lowered his eyes to meet hers, just as the word left his mouth.

"Yes. The traitor."

"And what business does a resident of the castle have with a traitorous murderer? At this hour?"

"What business do you have asking me what I'm doing? It's got nothing to do with you."

"why, of course it does. If you are here to conspire with a known traitor, and I were to let you in, it would be very much my concern."

"Yes, well, I'm not here to conspire, I'm just visiting my brother." Calia stopped herself.

"Brother?" said the guard, a wry smile growing on his face. "Well now I *am* concerned."

"I'm just here to see if he's OK."

"I can assure you that he is quite well, but he is not allowed visitors."

"No visitors? Why?" she was becoming visibly anxious.

"Isn't that obvious? A crime of this magnitude, the delicate nature of his situation?"

"Delicate?"

"Yes, very few know of your brother, nor the crimes that he has committed."

"Well, I do. And I would like to speak with him."

"I'm afraid that won't be possible."

"Not possible for me? Why?"

"Not possible for anyone."

Calia's tension was turning to anger.

"I shall come back here with one of the kings, and you will let me see him. Mark my words."

"Mark mine, young lady. You will not be able to visit your brother… king or no king. Now go, before I arrest you for treason." Calia had been in this situation before. The stubbornness of the new guards had been a close match for her. Her desire to see Viga only intensified at being refused access.

"Treason?" she asked, keeping her tone as civil as she could.

"Yes, conspiring with traitors is treason. It is as simple as that."

"Fine. Have it your way." She said, as she turned on her heels angrily. The guard smirked as she stomped off down the long, dark hallway, pushing her way past the other guards.

Outside, the candlelight continued to dance across the walls of the castle's vast halls. The music still played, louder than ever, and the people danced with unwavering joy and freedom. As the rest of the kingdom lost itself in hedonistic pleasure, Calia sat on a step and focused.

She had to find a way into the dungeon… she had to see him. He had been alone too long. She thought about interrupting the kings and asking for their assistance, but of all the times, this was not it. They would rightly instruct her to wait until tomorrow, but she knew that she could not. Once Calia got something in her mind, there could be no stopping her, even now.

The hallway leading to the dungeon was long and narrow, gradually sloping down to the lowest floor of the castle. There must have been at least ten guards lining it. One way in… and one way out. She thought long and hard about a diversion to distract the guards, but there were so many that it would be unlikely to distract them all. Even then, the only door was locked by one of possibly fifty keys; taking them from the guard was difficult, finding the right one in time would be impossible.

During Jori's reign, there had never been any mention of a dungeon. Insubordination was infrequent, and treason was unheard of… until Viga.

It was too late to ask for assistance. The cooks were fast asleep, any friend or acquaintance that she knew would be lost in the revelry that surrounded her, that deafened and suffocated her. The one person she would have been able to rely on for help in a situation like this was the one that she was so desperate to find. He may not have been the brightest, but he was always willing to help. As her thoughts turned to her brother once more, she suddenly remembered.

That's where she had seen that room before. The long, gradual slope of the hallway… the big, locked doors. It was the ale room. King Jori used to store his ale below the floor, rolling barrels up that long corridor. Calia was strong for her size, but no match for a barrel full of ale. The duty of pushing the barrels up the hallway was left to able bodied guards.

Viga had been unceremoniously removed from assisting with the ale barrels ever since he was found inside one of the

223

store rooms, drunk and asleep, after sneaking in to steal a bottle of cider each for them. Unbeknown to the King at the time, it was Calia who had helped Viga gain entry into the ale stores, holding a ladder for him to climb through a high window. Once he was inside, Viga abandoned his modest yet achievable mission of returning with two bottles, turning his attention instead to a much bigger reward. His silence with regard to Calia's assistance that night was an attempt to atone for his selfishness the night before, leaving Calia high and dry, holding an incriminating ladder.

That was it! The way in. So much had changed since the dungeon was a store room and there was no guarantee that the window was still in place. She could remember how high the window was, and at this hour had no access to a ladder. Calia was unstoppable when she had an idea, even more so when she had a plan. With everyone she knew either asleep or too busy enjoying themselves. In times like these, she always knew who to turn to.

Stealth was never a great talent of Astrus'. His abnormal size and great strength meant that he had never had much cause to sneak anywhere, and if he did it, would have little impact on concealing him. As Calia led him through the alleyways from the stables to the dungeon, Astrus did his best to stay hidden, shuffling his way through the narrow hallways and streets. Once they arrived at the back of the cells, Calia was filled with relief. The window was still there.

New windows now accompanied it, with heavy steel bars embedded into the stone walls. She pondered why a cell block would leave an open window intact, *surely an oversight?* She thought. As she got closer, she realised why... The window was far higher than she had remembered. She had not grown much since her youth, but from where she now stood, the window seemed impossibly high.

The foolish bravery of her youth had now abandoned her.

Calia nervously clambered up the long, outstretched neck of her beloved horse, as he grunted quietly beneath her. Once she was perched awkwardly on his head, he lurched forwards and stamped his giant hoofs on the wall below the window, allowing her to climb clumsily through. Holding tight onto Astrus' reigns, she lowered herself down to the floor and turned to find her brother.

The room was smaller than she expected. Three small, solid cells lined each wall of the former store room, each with a small hatch set at eye level in the heavy wooden doors. At the door, a large oil lamp flickered and filled the room with warm light. The window was just as high from inside, but with no friend to assist her escape. A stack of three empty crates sat next to the door of the first cell, used to carry items to and from the cells; not even close to giving her enough height to execute an escape. This was a problem she would have to solve, but she turned her thoughts back to Viga.

She crept forwards, no way of knowing which cell contained her brother.

"Viga" She whispered. Her voice was almost imperceptible. Too loud, and she would alert the guards, too quiet and Viga would not hear. *Too quiet*, she thought. As she approached the first cell, she slowly lifted a wooden crate and placed it in front of the door; eye level to guards and prisoners was not the same thing for Calia.

She slowly pulled back the small hatch and peered within. There was nothing. "Viga?" she whispered again in the same overly hushed tone. There was no reply. She moved on to the second door, carefully lifting the crate once more to

225

avoid making any unnecessary noise. As she looked cautiously through the hatch, her gaze was met by an elderly man, his hands weighed down to the floor with heavy chains. His hair and beard were long and grey and his clothes were dark and tattered. His eyes lit up at the sight of the two dark, shapely eyes staring back at him; an unexpected glimmer of beauty. He opened his mouth to greet her, but was cut short with a gentle "Shhhh." Calia held her finger to her lips and mouthed an apology to the elderly man.

With only one more door to go on this side of the room, she picked up her pace; she had already been here too long. Excitement started to course through her veins as she picked up the stool once more and placed in firmly at her feet. She climbed up and quickly but quietly pulled the hatch open.

Nothing could have prepared her for what lay before her in that cell. Viga's cold, vacant eyes glaring back at her as he hung limp and listless from the ceiling by his neck. All colour had long since left his body, as had his life.

36

ESCAPE

The noise flooded the small room and flowed rapidly up the long hallway. A blistering, animalistic scream that surprised even Calia, as it exploded from deep within her.

She stood frozen on her empty crate, her fingers gripping so tightly to the small hatch that they had turned white. That moment seemed to last forever. Her brothers' eyes bulged out of his head, his usual gormless, vacant expression replaced with horrific surprise. Her brief trance was broken suddenly by the clanging of armour outside the door. She could hear the nearest guard fumbled frantically through his keys, the others noisily clanging their way towards him. She knew what being caught would mean... the accusations that would follow.

The large wooden bar creaked its way up the heavy door, Calia hid, terrified behind the large oil lamp that stood next to the door. With a loud thud, the door slammed open and the guards rushed in, immediately filling the room. Calia had to act now. She pulled the lever on the large gas lamp swiftly, within a second, they were plunged into darkness. The room was a frenzy of clashing armour, confused shouting and frenetic scrambling.

She pushed behind the closest guard and ran out of the room into the dimly lit corridor, the mass of muddled guards turning behind her. She ran up the corridor, and dived under the feet of the last guard to attend the commotion. She was small, but not always agile. Limping from her ambitious dive, she hobbled quickly up the ramp and out into the castle.

She knew she could not outrun the guards, there were too many, and once they had turned and gathered themselves, they would have enough momentum to catch her. She had to hide. Her instinct was to retreat to her room, *there must be somewhere she could hide there?*

She pushed through the crowds of people in the spacious hall outside the dungeon and headed towards the staff quarters. As she reached the opening to the hallway that led to her room, she could hear the commotion as the guards forced their way through the crowds behind her. Screams and shouts grew closer as guards knocked down the unsuspecting revellers, forging their path towards her. She looked down her hallway to freedom, only to find two guards stationed at the end of the hall. The staff quarters were close to the halls where the public were amassed. If it were not for her current predicament, she would be glad that their rooms were being protected.

She needed another sanctuary, she could not seek refuge with the kings, as she would have to explain where she was and what she was doing. They had been generous to acquit her of any treason or collusion with her brother, this would only draw their attention back to her. The cooks were asleep, and overlooked by guards. The guards loudly entered the hall… she was running out of time.

There was only one place left. She crouched lower and doubled back on herself. She moved quickly and quietly through the crowds, trying not to draw any attention. The crowd was dense and provided good cover. She was not as conspicuous as the guards, but she stood out clearly from the rest of the party due to her simple, messy work clothes. As she neared the exit on the far side of the room, one of the guards looked back and caught sight of her.

"There! She's over there!" he shouted.

"Stop! Stop that girl!" shouted another. Calia lowered her head and ran, pushing her way forcefully through the oblivious strangers. Running up the corridor, her mind began to turn to the last time she had stepped through these halls. The only place left where she felt safe, her last refuge.

She had not walked up the hallways to Jori's room since he last inhabited it, she hadn't thought what would have happened to it, she could only hope that it was still there… still safe. The stairs that lead to the former king's quarters were longer than she recalled, she had not run this far in a long time and it was beginning to catch up with her. As the stairs spiralled in front her, she began to feel dizzy, but she did not have far to go.

Finally, at the top of the stairs, she doubled over onto her knees and caught her breath. Looking around the landing outside her beloved King's room, she saw that nothing had changed. A wave of relief washed over her. The landing was dark and empty, except for a statue of the King; an awkward gift for such a humble man, but he had appreciated the sentiment. The stone king stood guard outside his own room;

a prominent fixture, but not one that Jori had to endure looking at for any length of time.

Calia composed herself and approached the door. She carefully opened it, full of worry about what might lay within. If the ale store was now a dungeon, who knows what changes would lay before her.

The room was dark, but to her surprise, it was still the same. Not only the same, the room was untouched. The bed was unmade, the surfaces were dusty. A quick pang of guilt struck her, only to remind herself that this was no longer her duty. She had never seen the room so neglected, but at least it was the same. The same comforting smell, the same ornaments on the shelves; simple yet pleasant, just like him.

She pulled the chair away from his desk and wedged it up against his door... then lit the candle on his dresser, where it always had been. She scanned the room, looking for a suitable place to hide, only to catch a glimpse of a foreign object in the corner.

Calia had spent many hours in this room, tending to her king, starting and cleaning the fire, making the bed and clearing up after the untidy monarch. She knew every item in this room, and where it should go. The chest that sat in the corner was nothing less than conspicuous, a dark wooden box with ornate brass trim and fittings, sat next to his simple wooden dresser.

Calia knew that she had no time, she knew that it was too much risk, but she had to know what was inside. She rushed to the corner of the room and slid to her knees beside the chest, wincing from the effects of the dive she had attempted earlier. Despite her clear lack of time, she opened the lid slowly. Inside she found a surprising set of objects; an unusually short sword, a gold bracelet and a letter.

Only one of these things was of any use to her at this moment. Calia had spent some of her youth playing around in the yard with army recruits and had learnt the basics of swordsmanship. She was competent, and could best her more enthusiastic brother in a duel; a fact that he was not happy about at all, especially given his occasional military aspirations. Sword or not, she knew that she was no match for the group of armoured guards that hunted her.

She grabbed the handle of the unusual weapon and pulled. Nothing happened. It was as if it were set in concrete into the floor. She pulled as hard as she could, but could only raise it an inch. *Some use this is,* she thought. *A sword too short to swing and too heavy to lift... thank you Jori.*

As she lifted, she could hear the familiar chaotic sound of rustling armour and shouting, breathless guards as they made their way up the stairs towards Jori's door. Her time was shorter than ever, and she could not waste it attempting a feat of impossible strength, no matter how frustrating it was.

She grabbed the letter and stuffed it in her dress and held the bracelet briefly to admire it. It was a simple gold lattice that curved round into a bangle, at its centre was a dark green gem, glowing gently in the candlelight, reflecting more light back than seemed possible, drawing her gaze in an almost entrancing way. The jewel was set in a golden circle that sat on top of the bracelet. She had never been one for shiny, ornate jewellery, but there was something captivating about this bangle that convinced her to keep hold of it.

Bang.

They were here. The angry guards were beating the door and shouting to her.

"We know you're in there. Just come out now and put an end to this!"

"Open this door now, or we shall break it down!"

From the heavy thuds that echoed around the old man's room, she knew that they had already begun. She was out of time and had found no safe place to hide. She looked around the room once more and saw nothing. They would check the bed, the cupboards. She had spent so much time in this room, that she knew the futility in her search. There were no hidden entrances or exits to her knowledge, although that was exactly the type of thing Jori would have enjoyed. The room was simple and basic, nowhere to run... nowhere to hide. She looked at the window that she occasionally opened for the king. She knew how far it was above the ground outside, but she also knew that it was her only chance of escape.

BANG.

She looked back at the door and made her way nervously to the window. She opened it wide and stood on the ledge. Looking down, it was dark and hard to make out where she would land. The candlelight and mass of people below her made it hard to see. The height of the tower alone made any notions of a safe landing impossible. As she leaned further out of the window to get a better look, her body jerked back and her skin went cold. She steadied herself on the wooden window frame, still clutching onto the bracelet awkwardly.

BANG!

Her hands began to shake and her knees trembled beneath her. She knew what she must do, but she could not face what it would mean. *Is this it?* She thought. Her fingers were cold and wet with sweat, she was losing her grip.

CRACK.

For a hasty plan, the door had resisted the guards valiantly, but it had finally succumbed to the force of the armed men. The next charge would be their last. Calia perched on the windowsill, steadied herself and prepared to jump. She took a deep breath and put the bracelet on her wrist for safe keeping. A shiver ran down her spine.

CRASH!

The guards stumbled into the room behind her with haste and anger. Calia's heart sank. The time when she had needed it the most… her bravery had deserted her. She had always prided herself on being courageous and fearless, only to find out in her most desperate moment that this was not the case. Her head fell and she climbed slowly down from the ledge and accepted her fate as an accused traitor. Having seen what the consequences of this had been for her brother, she rued her lack of courage to jump even more than before.

"Where is she?" Said one of the guards, furiously opening cupboards.

"There was nowhere else that she could go! There is only one room at the top of those stairs." Said another.

"Did she definitely come up here? You are sure?"

"Of course, we all saw her."

This is no time for foolish games, she thought. The idea that they would play with her only added insult to the shame of being caught.

"There. She must have jumped out of the window." Said another guard, pointing to the open window.

"No sign of her. She wouldn't have, surely? That would certainly kill her."

"Well, then she has met her fate."

Calia stood next to Jori's bed, dumbfounded.

"And what do we tell the kings? It's not our place to force her to her death, they are the ones who must decide her fate."

"We say nothing. This didn't happen." Said the guard who she had confronted at the dungeon. "If the kings find out

that we let a young girl, not only break into the dungeon…
but escape us… what do you think that means for our jobs?"

Calia's legs began to shake again, she could not believe
her eyes. She watched bemused as the guards closed the
window and organised the former King's belongings. By the
time they had left the room and closed the door, her stomach
was in her mouth. She breathed slowly and lay down on Jori's
bed. She could not stay there, but she was not sure she could
walk. *What had happened?* She took out the letter from her
dress and read.

37

THE LETTER

My Dear Sons,

No doubt, you will find this letter while packing up my belongings. Held within this case are the two most powerful items in the entire kingdom and I give them, to you.

These two precious items were gifted to me by an ancient wizard named Falmond, after my time at the table of the Grand Council all those years ago. They possess within them, such strong magic that I dare not leave them free for anyone to wield. I'm sure that upon my demise, you will find this letter and take good care of them.

The first of these items is 'The Amulet of Serenity', it grants the wearer the ability to go completely unseen. I had the Amulet set into a bracelet that belonged to be beloved Lowena, that I placed a charm on. Only those who are pure of heart may wear the bracelet and therefore gain access to the powers of the amulet.

The second of these is 'Risu the Unstoppable', a blade that can cut through any object. From flesh, to steel and stone, this sword will slice through it with ease. Thankfully, during my reign I have never found cause to use this weapon, although at times it was of great use in the building of the nation that you rule over today. Like the amulet, this is protected with a powerful spell.

My knowledge of the ancient magic that I had witnessed all those years ago was limited, I had to spend a long time to get this right. It also required a great deal of my life force for me to make the magic work. You may remember me working on something in private, prior to my abdication. The sacrifice that it took from me almost killed me, and for a moment, I thought that it had.

I hope that you can understand my reasoning for placing such charms on these magical items, I simply could not risk them getting into the wrong hands. I am safe in the knowledge from what I have seen of the three of you that you will be more than capable of harnessing the power that they may grant, and that you will use this for the betterment of the nation that I have built.

A truly great leader must have the power to forge forward and the strength to enforce his will for the good of his people. He must also have the strength of mind to move unseen, to allow others to lead the way. Sometimes you must take charge, and sometimes you must lead from behind, letting others take the Helm. This is the way I have led throughout all these years, and it is my wish that you do the same.

You have all the power you need to become great kings. You can lead this Kingdom to great prosperity and happiness. Do not underestimate your people, in time you will come to see why I have involved them in the running of the kingdom alongside the three of you. This will grant you the knowledge and wisdom that allow you to weld this sword, and as long as your hearts stay pure, you may benefit from the great power that the amulet possesses.

Good luck my sons, my kings.

Jori.

Calia lay motionless, trying to take this in. She had heard of magic, but never experienced it for herself. She had been invisible, truly invisible. She could hardly comprehend how something like this could happen, especially to her. Her excitement soon gave way to guilt.

Have I stolen this? She thought, imagining Jori's disappointed face, his bushy eyebrows upturned and his soft eyes boring into her heart. She had seen this before, she knew how it felt. For as long as she could remember, her aim in her working life was simple… keep the king happy.

She slowly pushed herself up from the bed and shuffled towards the chest. She knelt beside it and opened the lid. The sword sat firmly at the bottom of the chest, supported by ark brown cloth. Looking down, she could feel the power of the sword, she could imagine what it was capable of… especially in the wrong hands. This weapon was intended for the kings, the kings who had just executed her brother.

An uneasy feeling filled Calia's body. Ever since the new kings had taken over, she had felt like she was moments from catastrophe, one step away from the blade. She wrapped the sword in the cloth that lay beneath it and closed the lid. She was tired, but she still had enough strength to pull the impossibly heavy chest over to Jori's bed. She pushed it the last few yards under his bed and draped his sheets over the side. It was all she could do for now. Putting the letter in her pocket, and holding the amulet tight, she scanned the room once more and then left for her quarters.

Printed in Great Britain
by Amazon